UNTHOLOGY 7

UNTHANK
BOOKS

First published in 2015
by Unthank Books

Printed in England by Imprint Digital UK

All Rights Reserved

A CIP record for this book is available from the British Library

Any resemblance to persons fictional or real who are living,
dead or undead is purely coincidental

ISBN 978-1-910061-12-1

Edited by Ashley Stokes and Robin Jones

Book and jacket design by Robot Mascot
www.robotmascot.co.uk

www.unthankbooks.com

CONTENTS

INTRODUCTION

The Editors

Fight Them? Astonish Us

We intended in this introduction to *Unthology 7* to reference
the first ten minutes of Jean Cocteau's *Orpheus,* in part because
the film features a literary journal called *Nudism*, an *Unthology*-
sounding title for a very un*Unthology*-like publication. *Nudism*
is full of blank pages.

The second reason for referencing *Orpheus* is something a
flat character says to Orpheus that struck us as profound and
perhaps has a bearing on our existential situation. However, we
became massively distracted by a short sequence sandwiched
between the appearance of *Nudism* and The Profound
Statement of the Flat Character: a highly enjoyable sub-scene
in which a lot of poets have a brawl in a bar. This sequence
could have continued for a lot longer. It could have been
extended to replace the rest of the film, if we're honest.

Rather than meshing *Nudism* and the Profound Statement of
the Flat Character into something that introduces *Unthology 7,*
we liked the poets' brawl so much (there is a lot of hair pulling)

that we instead started to toy with the idea of suggesting an Orpheus-Cocteau Stratagem to revive the UK's flagging pub industry. Pubs could provide 24-hour poet fights to pull in the punters. There could be tag team events, pro-am, side betting. A distinct new form of tic-tak could emerge among the bookies, which in turn the poets would adopt to construct new verses and rhymes. No one would ever get bored. They would hang around in pubs for longer and visit them more frequently and thus drink more beer and buy more bags of pork scratchings and Scampi Flavour Fries. This would cheer up a lot of publicans and help some poets get out more.

However, we thought we would get into trouble with the Nabob-State for saying this even in jest or a doomed gesture towards entrepreneurialism. Or we'd be taken so seriously that we'd be given a grant to develop what in the end would be just a new form of elite cockfighting or weasel baiting. It is possible, too, that some people might see this as a poet cull by stealth and Brian May would compose a song accompanied by a bad video that slags off *Unthology*. This wouldn't be fair as we've done some good things, too.

Anyway, back to *Orpheus*.

As the poets brawl, Orpheus says, 'What should I do? Fight them?'

The Flat Character, says, profoundly, 'Astonish us.'

Don't fight them. Astonish us.

We thought we could learn some tricks if we took this sentiment seriously instead of fantasising about poets fighting, if we stopped imagining all the kudos that would flow rightly to us if we revived the UK pub trade by means of semi-barbaric spectacle, if we started to inhabit the new reality for a just a minute or two.

Fearing we'd be told off, or that the whole thing would backfire and Brian May would get involved, we abandoned the idea of referencing Jean Cocteau's *Orpheus* even without a tangential description of the codification or legalization of the poets' brawl.

We entertained many other ways of introducing *Unthology 7*, from describing each of the stories and restating our editorial philosophy to help out hipster reviewers who struggle with the concept of eclecticism unless it's spelled out for them in simple terms. We considered interviewing ourselves in twee and mimsy fashion, staging a dialogue in which we tell you about how exquisite the writing we host here is; how luminous and talented our campus peer group; or how some spent-force puppet master says we're very nice people doing nice things for the nice people that he approves of and pay him homage. We thought hard about whether to use the introduction to *Unthology 7* to provide an august and lofty survey of something called the State of the Short Story, or use it to tell you that we're so middle class that we need no introduction. The gentry love us anyway and we have friends in the media so we're taking the summer off to lounge about somewhere where we don't have to bother ourselves with the writing of introductions. We even thought about having another rant about something popular but not very well written or interesting, or making up some more words with 'ism' at the end of them, because an anthology series needs a persona, and ours just happens to be a bit warped, contradictory and saddening.

But: Fight Them? Astonish Us.

In the end we decided to let *Unthology 7* stand for itself by cutting away all the absurd rhetoric and eager-to-be-misconstrued polemic. We would simply quote from its first offering, George Djuric's *The End May Justify the Means but Who Will Justify the End?*

Then we realized that we couldn't even do this. We would steal some of George's thunder.

We didn't want to steal any of George's thunder and in the end decided that *Unthology 7* would have to go without any introduction at all.

As ever, we are very apologetic for letting you down.

Over to you, George Djuric, fighter, astonisher.

THE END MAY JUSTIFY THE MEANS BUT WHO WILL JUSTIFY THE END?

George Djuric

Oscar Wilde walks through the customs, Anything to declare, sir? I declare I am a genius. I walk through the customs. Anything to declare, buddy? My name is George, you can buddy yourself, and all I have to declare is this memory of the slums I grew up in that I carry like a bible inside the pocket in front of my heart. Any tax on that, buddy?

The colour of one's creed, necktie, eyes, thoughts, manners, speech, is sure to meet somewhere in time of space with a fatal objection from a mob that hates that particular tone. And the more different, the more unusual the man, the nearer he is to the stake. There is nothing dictators hate so much as an unassailable, eternally elusive, eternally provoking gleam. One of the main reasons why the very gallant Russian poet Gumilev was put to death by Lenin's ruffians was that during the whole ordeal, in the prosecutor's dim office, in the torture house, in the winding corridors that led to the truck, in the truck that took him to the place of execution, and at that place itself, full of the shuffling feet of the clumsy and gloomy shooting squad, the poet kept smiling.

You never knew back then back there, some schmuck pulls a virtuoso knife out and it swiftly travels to deliver a cardiac arrest. Where I grew up it was a daily ritual, even though virtuoso knives were scarce. You walk through my Zemun neighborhood, and by the time you reach the end of the street, where gypsy shacks kiss a dump field, the infamous Yelovac, your pants are wet and your ass stinks, or it is them who double stink by now; no gray, scented area there. They stare you down, you stare back at them, that's the juice; unless some weak sucker can't handle his fear and he jumps at you screaming at the top of his lungs while trying to bury his void, or even better, fill it with an inflicted wound. If you've seen the *Gangs of New York*, you know how poetic it is compared to a never-ending bildungsroman of the slums; that is if you've ever tasted the actual slumslife. If not, hang in, you might learn a thing or three. Back then, probability of survival wasn't a mere computation of odds on the dice or more complicated variants; it was the acceptance of the lack of certainty in your capability to survive, and the development of methods for dealing with your survival.

Truth to be spitted out with a phlegm. While I was quite cross-eyed as a kid, my mind wasn't; I knew I had to step it up the first time around, otherwise I'd become their steady customer. I'm a six-year-old sent for a loaf of bread some three hundred yards down the street. I walk by the old houses worn smooth by the winds of innumerable days, with echoes and memories of colours scattered in the depth of the cloudless sky. A few more houses and the street ceases to maintain any pretence of urbanity, resembling a man returning to his little village who piece by piece strips off his Sunday best, slowly changing back into a peasant as he gets closer to his home.

The very first time I take upon this adventure, the Zemun's barbarians are there, with an expression which no human tongue can render any account of: a rigid, stern looks settled upon their features with a slight frown as if in response to some gloomy thoughts or unpleasant sensation; five scumbags playing soccer in front of the bunkered heavy metal gates of Navip, the biggest liquor and wine producer in Yugoslavia, its high walls featuring broken glass that blasts kaleidoscope reflections straight into my eyeballs. The shoddies shower me with names, curses, but I keep on going – intimidated, pissed, but not scared. Then they block the way, interrupting my mission: it is an obstacle I have to overcome, obstacle that gives the measure of a deed and of the man who performs it. I stop. Now what? After a verbal massage they let me go. To be repeated on my way back; this time they reach for my bread (no butter back then – one day a man walks in our yard looking for fresh sour cream since we had a cow: Say what?!). A rush of fear shakes my body as I hit the closest raider and break his slimy nose. He runs away weeping, the brave bunch follows; I storm home pressing the blood-stained bread on my chest. I feel free yet frightened – the first giaour to enter the forbidden city of Mecca. Few days later I go again. The pressure of the unknown boils inside my head: I can't wait to get over with it. They look at me, I look at them. No one says a freakin' word.

For my part I have no doubt as to the internal causes that led me to pen this episode – I do so under stress of a comparatively unusual but very powerful sentiment: that of shame. This first win, though, felt striking. Depending who you ask, it was like entering the Pink Floyd studio during the recording of the *Dark Side of the Moon*, or the first lap of the 24 Hours of Le Mans; or even juicier, a reading of *A Universal History of Infamy*. This book dumped on my barely literate shoulders the weight I wasn't ready for. As far as I could see there was no writing on the wall either – the walls were all shelved up from bottom to top, bearing the enormous pressure of the antimatter. Let us ad hoc call this collection of unread books an antilibrary. I don't think I've felt that much gravity ever after: my shoulders itch at this muscle reminiscence. And for the reason unknown to me, we all assume the matter to weigh more than antimatter, let alone the qualitative preferences we readily shower it with. I am by no means an expert when it comes to astrophysics, but I'll question any material arrogance.

Years later, driving my race car sideways through the very first curve of my first rally, still trying to get away from the slums as far and as fast, a voice spoke to me: One of these days the future will be here, and you won't be ready for it. Then it touched my shoulder and drifted away. The message became absolutely clear just feet away, when my Abarth overheated and the smell of the burning present filled the cockpit with fumes. My longtime obsession had the makings for disaster, which my feeble brain refused to recognize being fried from the frantic action.

The illusion of future is always at its best in the half-light of dawn or dusk. The sense of distance lacks: a ridge nearby can be a far-off mountain range, each small detail can take on the importance of a major variant on the countryside's repetitious theme. The coming of day promises a change; it is only when the day had fully arrived that the observer suspects it is the same day returned once again – the same day he has been living for a long time, over and over, still blindingly bright and untarnished by time. Whatever is a reality today, whatever you touch and believe in and that seems real for you today, is going to be, like the reality of yesterday, an illusion tomorrow.

Immediately when you arrive in the illusion, for the first or the tenth time, you notice the stillness. An incredible, absolute silence prevails inside that moment; even in busy places like the flea markets or whoretta sisterhoods, there is a hushed quality in the air, as if the quiet is a conscious force which, resenting the intrusion of sound, minimizes and disperses sound straightaway. Then there is the sky, compared to which all other skies seem fainthearted efforts. Solid and luminous, it is always the focal point of the landscape. At sunset, the precise, curved shadow of the earth rises into it swiftly from the horizon, cutting into light section and dark section. When all daylight is gone, and the space is thick with stars, it is still of an intense and burning blue, darkest directly overhead and paling toward the earth, so that the night never really goes dark.

At this point you will either snap and hurry back inside the slums, or you will go on standing there and let something very peculiar happen to you, something that everyone who lives in the myth has undergone and which the French call *le bapteme de solitude.* It is a unique sensation, and it has nothing to do with loneliness, for loneliness presupposes memory. Here in this wholly antimaterial landscape lighted by stars like flares, even memory disappears; a strange, and by no means pleasant process of reintegration begins inside you, and you have the choice of fighting against it, and insisting on remaining the person you have always been, or letting it take its course. For no one who has stayed in the myth for a while is quite the same as when he came. Of course, no matter how keenly an epiphany is presented and analyzed, there will be minds that remain blank and spines that remain unkindled.

Perhaps the logical question to ask at this point is: why this obsession with future, this addiction to myth? The answer is that when a man has been there and undergone the baptism of solitude he can't help himself. Once he has been under the spell of the vast luminous, silent country, no other place is quite strong enough for him, no other surroundings can provide the supremely satisfying sensation of existing in the midst of something that is absolute. He will go back, whatever the cost in time or money, for the absolute has no price.

The map I am using today does not feature the village of Zemun, nor it pinpoints the Sime Šolaje Street as it fades into the deep dump. Doesn't even indicate the vast area of my beloved slums, still religiously placed in front of my aging heart. How very inconsiderate on the part of the cartographers, I'll bet they didn't forget to indicate their own shitty hometowns, those illiterate morons. Which clearly indicates how unsustainable the past is, a fishing trip delusion entirely surrounded by liars in old clothes. Which leaves the mythology as the last and only asylum available to the man of reason, or the woman of vanity: My dear Dorianna, you don't dye your hair to deceive other people, or to fool yourself, but rather to cheat the picture in your closet a little.

What is the myth after all if not the most authentic ending which is already revolving towards another beginning. Let me bless those soccer playing freaks, for in the natural evolution of things the ape would perhaps never have become man had not a freak appeared in the family – direct opposite to when a writer is born into a family, then the family is finished. But there, everything has its drawbacks, as the man said when his mother-in-law died, and they came down upon him for the funeral expenses. After all, the '60s are gone, dope will never be as cheap, sex never as free, and the rock never as great.

I recently wrote about the editorial analysis (I still deny my temptation to embrace this *analysis* with quotation marks) I received from a literary magazine in regards to one of my submitted illusions, and at this juncture I have to quote a tiny bit of it: 'Why would a library full of books be considered *the* wonder of the world...?' It's probably me, but I'm missing something here. Name any other *wonder* of the world, and I'll laugh at the comparison.

Going to work, on the other hand, is yet another myth from the tedious library of Karl Marx. At aged six I wasn't philosophically inclined: I hoped for a life spent in the labyrinth of my own fantasies, fantasies constructed of other minds' labyrinths – anything that would isolate me from mental ubiquity of the slums surrounding the farm my grandfather had, from those names my peers slammed over my large head and my refreshing Marty Feldman stare. Two eye surgeries and the relocation to the capitol took care of my exterior troubles, leaving the usual interior suspects to the Ministry of Home Affairs i.e. behind the bars, letting them feed, like a jackal, among the tombstones.

I still can't even figure out why I walked away from my propitious racing career. I was at my peak, only 21 years old, just a tad shy of the full-fledged mastery in terms of driving technique; but the speed was there: I broke almost every single record in the class. And walked away. I can't extract the crucial turning catalyst which irrevocably overpowered all the reason shouting within me. It could've been some unknown personal trait that kicked in *de profundis*, or that Slavic self-destructive impulse.

One clue remains certain: George and I haven't been on the best of terms ever since. There was a mortal leak of antimatter, which kept cutting my future peaks half-mast, an absence of the secret ingredient that made alchemists amaranthine and philosophers tangible. For a brief, flickering moment George had it lined up, and as I walk away from him in disbelief, he is where he always wanted to be: racing his bolide through the labyrinth of what-could've-beens.

Now I will have to conceive of other things, which is an equivalent of Now what?! All my troubles didn't start in Teba Hecatompilos, that was Borges's Alamo, but in a similar place: a local library. I was five years old when my aunt took me there and pointed at the wonder of the world. I don't think I was that much of an asshole back then, maybe an asshole's apprentice, so my scream had sincerity written all over it: 'But what am I going to read once I'm done with these books?!' My dear aunt wasn't on par with the question, so my very first existential incertitude went uncomforted.

Even at this early age of mine I could clearly see the traces of betrayal, a foggish abbreviation from the path of genius: reading made me too comfortable from the get-go, always a bad omen. I built a self-sustained universe, a parallel reality; the more furnished that castle became, the less appealing outdoors activities reflected in my binoculars. Then the winter would come, as it does once a year, and my father, grandpa, uncle Brne, and uncle Žika would wrestle a three hundred pound hog in the yard and slice its throat open, shattering my shelter into pieces and leaving me bare naked in the frost.

Not understanding yesterday guarantees understanding tomorrow even less, today the least. The future will, as it usually does, produce its own new fallacies, regardless of the fact that they will be the same as ours, as old as the world, which won't prevent our grandkids from being proud of them, wiping their asses with our old fashioned wisdom in the process. The place will smell of fairgrounds, of lazy crowds, of nights when you stayed out because you couldn't go to bed, and it will smell like New York, of its calm and brutal indifference. Those will be the most monotonous fuckin' crickets I ever heard in my life, since anticipation is a very subjective affair. Just like a man grieving because he has recently lost in his dreams the confidence he had never had in reality, hoping tomorrow he would dream that he found it again. That is how the myth is created; it has its fatal flaw: in the evening the Nevsky Prospect is illuminated by electricity. While in the daytime the Nevsky Prospect needs no illumination.

It took me ages, some forty years since my first novel hit the furnace, to realize why I quit rally racing. In the meantime I became an expert on the subject of *toska*. No single word in English renders all the shades of *toska*. At its deepest and most painful, it is a sensation of great spiritual anguish, often without any specific cause. At less morbid levels it is a dull ache of the soul, a longing with nothing to long for, a sick pining, a vague restlessness, mental throes, yearning. In particular cases it may be the desire for somebody of something specific, nostalgia, love-sickness. At the lowest level it grades into ennui, boredom. Not in my case scenario, though: I explored every possible debilitating option within alienated labour, mostly selling cars across the Southern California dealer network, from Toyotas to Nissans, then Fords and BMWs, Hondas too. The only thing I can recommend at this stage is a sense of humour. Meanwhile time went about its immemorial work of making me look and feel like shit. I didn't care; always busy with a new carrot a foot away, bigger and juicier by every new occasion, I'd dream of being promoted into sales management, then becoming a real estate tycoon, the stock market guru. Until one not so fine day we lost our house of thirteen years, which drew the line in the sand for me, sending Eileen and my pitiful self to where the actual sand is – Desert Hot Springs, California. At that point the final *Now what*?! happened to be in the tough neighbourhood of ours, considering the 2009 reputation of this crime infested shoottown. Back in the slums!

Some idiots never learn, some learn the first time; I explore, while Eileen pays the bill. I'll let you in the deepest secret of mine: I'm going to join the duo, make it the three tenors: what did Nabokov and Joyce have in common, apart from the poor teeth and the great prose? Exile, and decades of near pauperism. A compulsive tendency to overtip. An uxoriousness that their wives deservedly inspired. More than that, they both lived their lives 'beautifully' – not in any Jamesian sense (where, besides, ferocious solvency would have been a prerequisite), but in the droll fortitude of their perseverance. They got the work done, with style.

All the emotional information I've had about myself to date is from forged documents. After this brand spanking sparkly resolution my doubts have their own private way of understanding each other, of becoming intimate, while my external person is still trapped in the commerce of ordinary words, in the slavery of car sales rules. The moment of truth, the sudden emergence of a new insight, is an act of intuition. Such intuitions give the appearance of miraculous flushes, or short-circuits of reasoning. In fact they may be likened to an immersed chain, of which only the beginning and the end are visible above the surface of consciousness. The diver vanishes at one end of the chain and comes up at the other end, guided by invisible links.

Well, I reappeared on the other side of the myth four decades later, as a writer. There is nothing truer than myth: history, in its attempt to 'realize' myth, distorts it, stops halfway; when history claims to have 'succeeded,' this is nothing but bullshit and mystification. Everything we dream is realizable, why not? Reality doesn't have *to be*, it is simply what it is. The greater danger for most of us lies not in setting our aim too high and falling short, but in setting our aim too low and achieving our mark. One arrives at style only with atrocious effort, with fanatical and devoted stubbornness, it's that simple. Magic is believing in yourself, if you can do that, you can make anything happen. What I am aiming at is an immobile movement, something which would be the equivalent of what is called the eloquence of silence, or what St. John of the Cross, I think it was him, describes with the term 'mute music.' And if anyone is reckless enough to question my credentials, she or he better speak now while I have a doubt or two, or forever shut up: Listen, I built this dream up from nothing. When I started all there was were slums. Other freaks said I was asinine to build myself up from the dump, but I started the construction all the same, just to show them. My racing career sank into that fuckin' dump. Then I built my business career. That sank there as well. So finally I built a temple of the finest illusions, a perfection. That one burned down in the desert heat, fell over, then sank into the dump. But this one... stayed up! And that's what you're going to get, ladies and gentlemen, an undisputable fictional alchemy for the salient taste of the 21st century.

Being a writer, I am are outside life, I am above life, I have miseries which the ordinary man does not know; I exceed the normal level, and it is for this that simple minds refuse to forgive me: I poison their simple peace of mind, I undermine their stability. I have irrepressible pains whose essence is to be inadaptable to any known state, indescribable in words. I have recurrent and shifting pains, incurable pains, the worst possible pains this side of malignant cancer, pains neither of the body nor of the soul but which devour both. No one has ever written, painted, sculpted, modeled, built, or invented except literally to get out of hell. Everything else is vanity, a fight between two bald men over a comb.*

*A word of caution: a masterpiece of fiction is an original world and as such is not likely to fit the world of the reader. If a writer is crazy enough to go about destroying literature, the reader has no choice but become an accomplice. She or he may not be interested in belletristic destruction, but destruction is interested in them. The end may justify the means as long as there is the reader to justify the end.

DEATH AND THE ARCHITECT

Roisín O'Donnell

I lost track of time and she darted away from me down a dark Barcelona street. My top hat flipped off my head and my coat was a swallow's tail behind me as I ran to keep up with her. I glimpsed time's impish face smiling as she ducked behind the shoulder of a six-winged gargoyle. And thus it began.

I searched for time down every damp alley in the *Barri Gotic*, where ivy leaves drip from rusty balconies, and shadows splinter in the crevices of the gothic cathedral. I pursued time around each corner of *El Raval,* where ladies of the night beckoned me with their coy bosoms and dangerous eyes, stroking my beard and enquiring if they could provide a little something of what I was looking for? In their tarnished pendants, I saw my own refection; a sincere Nordic face with a dandy's moustache and eyes of overly-ambitious blue. Turning from those tempting lips I struggled up the spine of *La Rambla* and I trekked the tree-lined boulevards of *Eixample.* As daylight faded, with burning bones I searched the pine-needled stillness of the *Mont Juic* forests. But time remained elusive, and I could only hear her whispering somewhere just beyond my dreams.

On impulse one night, I caught the train out to the town of Vic to seek the wisdom of my old friend Padre Josep. As I waited for my friend to finish saying the evening mass, I studied the famous frescos of Vic Cathedral, which offer an exhaustive menu of ways in which to spend ones time in hell. The devil's face in the painting above my head had the tantalising snarl of Señor Rogent when he handed me my architect's diploma, *'We have given this academic scroll to either a mad man or a genius... time will tell.'* From floor to ceiling the tortured bodies of the saints writhed and twisted. San Antonío knelt with his body porcupined by arrows. Santa Lucia uncomplainingly held her own eyes on a plate.

'Good to see you, Señor Gaudí.' Padre Josep kissed my cheek and we stepped outside the cathedral into a foggy, farm-smelling street. I could hear time giggling like a schoolgirl somewhere close by, and the mist amplified and distorted her every echo. Gas lamps shone ethereal through the haze, from which passers-by emerged like startled spirits. We ducked into a tavern on the porticoed *Placa Major*, where I explained to Josep the problems I was currently experiencing with time. The priest chuckled and stirred his *cortado*. 'Time is no man's friend, Señor Gaudí... And she'll wait for no man either.'

'So how am I meant to track down time?' I asked him.
Padre Josep smiled. 'My dear Antoní... Only God has a handle on time. God and nature. For they alone are infinite.'

Worried by these words, I fasted myself into a wholly intentional delirium. In my feverish dreams that night, the dark-haired Josefa Moreu was telling me she loved me, but I was distracted because I saw time peeping from behind the wizened wish-bone branches of the two trees in front of our family home in *Riudoms*. 'I love you like the sun, the moon, the stars,' Josefa said. 'I love you like the ocean,' she said. But I didn't reply because I was too busy watching time, determined not to let her out of my sight on this occasion.

My young niece Rosa tempted me out of my starvation with rustling bags of roasted *castanyes* and soft marzipan *panallets*.

In the sweet-smelling dusk of our turreted Barcelona house, I'd show Rosa my latest architectural drawings and tell her about my hunt for time, while Papa frowned silently from his armchair by the fireplace. By day I busied myself by designing some odd-legged chairs for Señor Güell, and I drew the altar for the monastery at Monserrat. Then with a stroke of either luck or genius, I decided to make a trap for time by securing the commission to design *a really big church*.

'It's going to be a temple, Señorita Moreu,' I told Josefa when we met for afternoon tea at the *Hotel Eixample*. Josefa fidgeted with her prim lace collar and checked her slim gold watch. Unlike my dream version of Josefa, the real Josefa wouldn't look into my eyes, and I was left staring at pieces of her, like the tiny mole under her left ear and the cup of shadow at the base of her neck. I showed her del Villar's blueprints for *La Sagrada Famila*, which I had drawn over with firm black ink, and Josefa's lashes lowered in concern. 'But…what's this Señor Gaudí?' she asked, indicating the curving spectacle of the central nave.

'It's inspired by nature, Señorita Moreu,' I told her, 'so it won't be dark and full of torment like those other churches. Joyous nature in her abundance has informed every element of the design… look here… see the wonderful curve of the pillars… like branches.'

'But church pillars are *straight*, Señor,' Josefa said, touching the pearls at her neck.

'Yes… but there are no straight lines in nature, Señorita Moreu,' I told her, hearing the twang of desperation in my voice and feeling the tug of Josefa's affection receding from me, like the tide rushing away from a shore. Just at that moment, time went gaily gliding past the window on a yellow unicycle and blew a kiss at me. I looked away.

Shortly after that, Josefa stopped replying to my letters. I started to pray the rosary three times per day, to attend mass in the gothic cathedral every noon and to fast on Mondays and Fridays. I designed *Casa Mila* with its wave-like façade, seaweed balconies, lily-pad flooring and spiralling cockle-shell staircases. I built *Casa Batalló* with its undulating sand-dune roof, which I brightened with smashed up ceramic tiles into a feast of colour. One sweltering June day as I worked on the meandering sea-serpent in *Park Güell*, I felt time running her cool fingers along my earlobes, and I kept my dear friend Padre Josep's words in my head, *'Remember Antoni, only God and nature are infinite...'*

DEAR SEÑOR GAUDÍ, ONCE AGAIN YOU HAVE EXCEEDED CITY LIMITS AND WE, THE COUNCILLORS, ARE OBLIGED TO TELL YOU TO STOP. THE CITY OF BARCELONA WILL NO LONGER PERMIT YOUR WILD FLIGHTS OF FANCY TO SCAR OUR CITYSCAPE. IT MUST STOP. IN FACT, WE REMIND YOU THAT WE ONLY EVER ASKED YOU TO DESIGN THE STREET LAMPS IN *PLACA REIAL*, AND LOOK WHAT HAPPENED ON THAT OCCASSION. DID WE ASK FOR FLOWERS? NO. DID WE ASK FOR LIZARDS? NO. DID WE ASK FOR A SOLDIER'S HELMET WITH A SNAKE COILING ROUND IT AND DISECTED EAGLES WINGS GROWING OUT OF IT? NO! NOW WE ARE ASKING YOU, SEÑOR, TO DO THIS CITY A FAVOUR AND JUST *STICK TO THE BLOODY PLANS!*

Long after Josefa's hesitant glances were but a memory, and both Rosa and Papa were gone from this life, I moved into my workshop in the crypt of *La Sagrada Familia*, where I lived and breathed amongst the dust of my creation. I prayed the rosary nine times per day. I fasted each weekday from dawn until dusk. I even threw away my smart coats and tried dressing in rags and growing a long matted beard so that time would mistake me for a beggar and pester somebody else. But it was all to no avail. Time continued to mock me relentlessly.

Occasionally some councillors would come down the steps to stick their top hats around the doorway of the crypt and cough, 'Ahem… Señor Gaudí?… Do you have eh… a completion date… roughly… in mind?'

My answer to them was always the same. 'My client, Señors, is God…. And as far as I am aware He is not in any hurry.'

Really it was only the apprentices who knew, or had guessed, how long this project would take. I saw the weight of lifetimes carried in each man's eyes. I sensed a heaviness about their limbs and I realised then that time had chained herself around their necks and was taking gleeful piggybacks on each mans' shoulders. Shocked by the blatant rudeness of time's behaviour, I would slam things down and throw things about and shout a lot to try and scare her away. I soon got a name for being short-tempered, which was unfair really.

At some point in the early twentieth century, I died. You'd think that dying would be something a person would remember. That it would stand out from other memories of breathless autumnal strolls in *Parc de Besos* with Josefa, or the day I threw a plaster-of-Paris jug at that young apprentice Jaime because he had ruined all the ultramarine tiling on the balustrade. But I have to admit that I have no recollection of dying at all. I can only suppose that it must have happened shortly after I got hit by that tramcar on *Corts Catalanes*. However I didn't waste too much time worrying about this, because I soon discovered that when a person is trying to catch something that is impossible to catch (like time) there are distinct advantages to being dead.

Now I was able to pounce on time as she lay asleep on the steps of *Mirador de Colón,* or swipe at her while she was teasing the salty-fingered fishmongers in the *Boqueriea* market. But I could never quite catch her, and in an infallible counter-move, time had a tantrum and blew herself up in the middle of Spain, halting building work on *La Sagrada Familia* indefinitely. Then, in an admittedly brilliant follow-up, time detonated herself in the centre of Europe, starting a world war which put construction of my basilica on hold for more than a decade. Not content with these initial sabotage attempts, time then destroyed my original models and plans, staged six acts of deliberate arson and two lootings, hired three inept architects and placed my church on the main route of a high-speed underground railway.

And yet my stone-winged phoenix continues to struggle from the ashes like the human castles of Tarragona summers, where the *pinya* weave their arms tightly together, as the tiny *enxaneta* climbs to the top, and the crowd gasps, wondering if she's going to fall. These days tourists line up around the block for a chance to step inside my uncompleted church. Sometimes I spot time standing in the entrance queues, licking a 99 ice-cream, wearing a *Barca FC* baseball cap, or posing for photographs with American families. Occasionally she waves or sticks her tongue out at me, but as soon as I step closer she disappears behind the plump limestone arse of a singing cherub.

'Why don't you give it up, Tio Antoní?' Rosa asked me as we sat together in the fronds of an unkempt palm. But I just shook my head.

It is incompleteness that fascinates us. Poles never reached. Liners lost mid-ocean. Hands almost held. Skins almost touched. Nearly completed spires paused on their ascent into the Barcelona sky. And a church under construction for more than a century. 'When will it be complete?' the tourists are always asking. But only time will tell, and she for the moment is jumping up and down on the yellow cranes surrounding the basilica, trying to get them to break. Meanwhile I wait, drifting in and out of shadows, sitting on the mosaic salamander in *Park Güell* or resting my aching bones on the glittering dragons' scale terrace of *Casa Batalló*.

SPIDERS

David Martin

Ten am, and the piledriver behind Rhys's eyes shows no sign of mercy. Beyond the safety glass, caverns of empty air tumble down and out to where the edge of the city is lost in the murk. The figures on the screen pulse and phase with the hideous internal rhythm of his stinking hangover. Bollocks to it, he thinks. He removes his headphones and looks around the vast open-plan.

'Mate, you look like shit.'

Rhys can only manage a grunt in response to Rich Walker. He may have initiated yesterday's ritual of post-work beers and grim speculation about who was next for the chop, but the horribly chipper Walker seems immune to hangovers. Rhys, however, had to get off the train two stops early this morning to barf in a bin, and only two espressos and a bottle of water have kept him upright through this first endless hour in the office. Calling in sick would have been a bad move. Only just scraping in for nine was risky enough with the axe swinging freely. Walker, mercifully, is distracted by something outside the window.

'Now that's a bad sign.' 'What is?' 'Looks like the window cleaners have got the boot as well. Look at that big bugger.'

Rhys has no idea what he's on about until he sees the thread stretched outside the window at the end of their row of desks, twenty-three floors up. A dark blob is crawling outside the pane, articulated legs shuttling along the filament that sways heavily under its weight. He notices two more spiders static and observant at the top of the glass. And he sees more of the web now, the larder of flies stuck and trussed in it.

'How the hell did they get up here?' Walker asks.

Rhys has no idea and doesn't want to think about the sheer cliff of metal and glass the spider is steadily traversing, or the air currents that pluck at those fragile threads. He gets up and heads for the kitchen, feeling the building heave in great queasy waves. He's not surprised the window cleaners have got the boot. Everything is falling apart, mirroring the company's fortunes. At least two of the lifts are permanently out of order, any kind of cleaner is a rare visitor.

The windowless kitchen is dangerously close to Niall's office, but feels more stable, away from the vertiginous edges. The whiff of stale milk from within the fridge doesn't help but Rhys braves it for the sake of the cup of tea that is rapidly becoming a matter of life and death. He roots about among the half empty cartons, markered with the usual warnings to the light-fingered. He wonders if this same scene is repeated in every office of every organisation, however prestigious, however feared. There was probably a pathetic fridge exactly like this in Hitler's bunker, Goebbels's semi-skimmed angrily labelled 'Hands Off!'.

When Rhys returns the spiders have crawled up out of sight. He can see now that the web continues all along the side of this floor. The hot tea begins its damage control work.

*

Homeward bound, knackered but knowing he is under an hour from the blessed collapse on the sofa, Rhys knows something's wrong the moment he steps off the underground. The dynamics of the crowd are all wrong, too much disorganisation in their movements for the usual disciplined rush of expert commuters turning in formation.

His suspicions are confirmed, the emergency warnings are flashing and the overground station is shut. Another bomb scare.

Emerging into the open air, the crowd jams pavements and spills into the road, hailing taxis. Police vans hoot their way through, a handful of fluorescent jackets try to direct gouts of humanity spurting out of the city's ruptured systems.

He hears it first, the unmistakable sound of something bad happening.

First a muffled shout, then a thud, hard momentum on bone, the sound of a body being broken, in that minuscule window of time before the screaming starts. An engine accelerates hard and he feels the car's shockwave through the air. Horns are sounding; there are shouts for help. The fluorescent jackets pass at a run.

The crowd hangs back, making space. The road clears around the man, deadweight on the tarmac, his face upturned, his eyes frozen at the instant of registering the car accelerating deliberately at him. Everything hangs suspended for a moment then collapses into a swarm of voices.

Rhys finally gets home to silence. He'd barely noticed his journey through the sprawling southern suburbs, the final tram ride; all the way the dead man's open eyes and shattered, useless limbs fill his exhausted mind.

The story of his day goes unspoken. Ruth hasn't returned. Everything is exactly where he left it, which he thinks may be the strangest thing after years of sharing space with someone else, their unpredictable activity and their unknowable motivations. He can't even smell any lingering trace of her, though her books still fill the shelves and all around him the dust is their mingled skin cells. He takes out his phone but can't bring himself to call.

He wakes once in the night and feels dread crawling like tar. He'd dreamt of hanging from that great glass and steel cliff, fingertips white with strain wedged into the frictionless crevices between the panes, nothing beneath his feet but the shattering drop.

*

It is dark behind the glass, the city a sea of orange sodium light, refracted in the overcast. Rhys is at his desk, virtually alone here. He's on the night shift, showing willing. The numbers don't sleep, the data entwines and powers the world outside, carrying messages of billions won and lost. The office takes on a bunker-like quality, the glow of the city reinforcing that hallucinatory tiredness of people who will next see the sun when it climbs back around from where it's currently driving sweat from the armpits of yelling traders on the dealing floors in Hong Kong and Tokyo.

As far as anybody understands it, this company used to be some unremarkable support function spun out from something that used to be a bank – something that is now lurching on in a zombie afterlife while slowly collapsing under the weight of its own impossibility, the shockwave deflected through mazes of dummy companies and offshore accounts, but still unstoppable. Its current ownership, and that of the building itself, is hazy. It produces fragments of software for a project whose purpose no one can quite remember. Maybe, somewhere out there, it will be one of its own long-forgotten subroutines, labouring to impose rules on to chaos, which finally notices the company's anomalous existence and terminates it.

Rhys feels like he's traversing the dark side of the moon, a trillion tons of frozen rock cutting him off from the world. At night, at least, all the options of the day are closed, and merely making it through the long haul to morning feels like an achievement.

There was a guy who used to work at the desk next to him. Lyndon, a thirty-something divorcee Rhys grudgingly admired for his convictions. He openly hated work and had as little to do with anyone as possible, in case he was sucked in and it did him permanent spiritual damage.

Then, about six months ago there had been a pronounced change in Lyndon. He seemed agitated, you could tell he was listening in to people's conversations rather than studiously ignoring them. At times he seemed on the verge of saying something then drawing back.

Rhys occasionally tried to make small talk and, as ever, his efforts were met with curt, functional responses. But Lyndon's eyes were desperate. Soon after that, he stopped coming in. Rhys later found out from a guy in HR that he'd been sacked after a stash of pornography was discovered on his machine.

No one knew what had happened to Lyndon. Rhys suspected that whatever the one thing had been that set him scornfully apart, a lover, a circle of friends, whatever he was secretly writing in his garret, had gone horribly wrong. His own defensive structures now imprisoned him in a vicious spiral of decaying confidence. He got lost.

Rhys wonders what had become of him. He imagines Lyndon staring at the ceiling of his bedsit, paralysed by his own fears, his world contracted to four walls.

*

'Ballooning,' says Walker triumphantly.

'Eh?'

'Ballooning. That's how the little bastards got there. They put out some silk like they were going to make a web. You get a massive updraft off a building like this so if you get it right you can float as high as you like. You'll probably end up dead. But if you land in a good spot, that draught keeps bringing all kinds of little insects up. Those lucky sods outside just sit there getting fatter and the food just keeps on coming right to them. The internet, mate. It's not just for porn, you know. Bloody hell you look rough.'

Rhys, hungover again, recoils from the lattice of over-familiar faces.

There is no disguising it. I have nothing to say to these people.

The clarity of the thought cuts through the blood roar and headache fuzz like shards of glass falling from the twenty-third floor.

The day's tension, and the tension of the days before that and back as far as he can remember, pour off his body. Sweat breaks out under his stiff new shirt. He can feel himself collapse into a cloud of buzzing black dots.

Outside, that tough little ecosystem was still thriving in the cracks of the building's carapace. However the colony had made it to this height, that tough little ecosystem was still thriving in the cracks of the building's carapace. Rituals hardwired since the Triassic had turned the window into a remarkably effective death factory for lesser lifeforms which, captured and wrapped, awaited their turn for dismemberment, dissolving in acid secretions and a slow pitiless devouring.

One day there'd been about ten spiders, the next only three big ones. Perhaps some dispassionate battle for supremacy had ended in cannibalism. Or maybe the weaker ones had only been defenestrated. Perhaps they'd floated down to ground level to begin the slow and steady climb back up for a revenge served stone cold.

'There'll just be one huge one left,' jokes Niall. 'One huge bugger that's eaten all the others up.'

Niall's left his office to come and wander aimlessly around the depleted floor that he used to believe he ran, staring at the spiders and trying to make lame conversation with the remaining staff. This is worrying in itself.

Rhys can't handle Niall's presence, so he heads for the increasingly feral gents' loo and locks himself in his favourite cubicle. And how sad is that, he thinks, to look forward to a few moments' solitude between MDF partitions, the plastic seat leaving its imprint in your pallid arse cheeks, your colleagues straining and farting a few inches away, the muffled airbursts and splashes. Rhys gazes down at his shoes between his bare thighs. Then the lights go out.

Only for a few seconds though. They flicker back on before causing anything more than a few theatrical squeals and laughs to filter through from the office.

He smiles, amused by his own momentary sense of excitement. That pretty much sums things up, he thinks.

*

No one saw Niall go, but his office stands shockingly empty, blinds wide open, stripped bare for a couple of days. Finally Louise, a rarely-sighted regional manager, painfully groomed and gym-tightened in a world of beer bellies and bad shaves, appears with a couple of nervous, shiny young men of indeterminate function and summons the survivors. She enthuses fearfully about the opportunities ahead, the new investors, the new boss they've sent in to shake the place up.

The next day, the blinds are shut but watchful, the new boss's presence fills the room, but he or she does not venture out.

Rhys keeps his head down for a few days, cutting down on the booze. At home he even occasionally sleeps in his own bed rather than falling asleep on the TV-lit sofa in the early hours. At work all conversations are snatched, clockwatching exchanges. Fear and worry is a constant background hum like faulty air con or the wifi finally starting to microwave your grey matter. Hardly anyone wants a pint and if they do the conversations are punctuated with long stares into space, eyes seeing bills, mortgage demands, children's faces. And sometimes they're seeing as though for the first time the desolate estates that surround the building's footprint, which the commuter trains sweep through without stopping.

Leaving the office late one evening, Rhys notices the window cleaners still haven't been. The pattern of webs has grown increasingly complex and the sinking evening sun is making it more visible; the summer that he'd barely registered is collapsing into autumn. He wonders if he'd be cut out for a career dangling in a cradle from a skyscraper and shivers at the thought.

One filament of web is shining almost gold in the sun as it heads away from the building at a strange angle. He realises it points out into the void of air towards the neighbouring tower, hundreds of metres away. He strains his eyes to follow its track, but can't for more than a few inches. Then he realises there's another. There are several shining tracks heading out at the same angle, into that impossible gulf. He stares for a while at the other tower. He imagines it suddenly flaring silver beneath a net of webs, an outpost of a hidden city that stretches from tower to tower unseen from the streets below, built from threads trembling with complex codes of vibrations and chemical signatures, reading the air currents, humming with its own inscrutable data.

As he makes his way from the tram stop he sees the car parked up on the kerb, boot open, his front door standing open. Ruth's back is turned as she loads a last cardboard box. A man Rhys hasn't seen before is emerging from the door, locking it. Rhys steps into the shadows of a shop doorway. He watches them stand together as the man shuts the boot, something conspiratorial in their stance says they are the new centre of a story whose murky fringes he's already being relegated to.

He remembers waiting for Ruth one evening, years ago, in the shopping plaza beneath her office tower. He'd sat on a low metal bench at 5pm, watching people steadily being extruded from the doors beneath the company logos, a wave front that rapidly built up and rushed towards him, breaking either side at the last moment, a sea of black and grey, patterns recurring, faces like computer-generated extras in a film. And he remembers seeing her the moment she emerged from the doors, standing out in all that rush. She was walking slowly, breaking the pattern, in that moment unaware of the surging crowd, looking only for him. The car door slams. Rhys ducks quickly across the street and into the off-licence.

*

He feels a deep sense of relief, of surrender to the inevitable. When he steps into the open-plan, unshaven and ashen faced, people avoid his eyes or exchange the briefest apologetic smiles. Even Walker doesn't ask where the hell he's been for the last three days. The summons is sitting as expected at the top of his stack of unread messages. All eyes follow his back and then duck sheepishly as he walks the length of the room and into the new boss's office. The door closes quietly behind, shutting out the rubbernecking stares and fearful whispers.

The gloom inside is thick, the blinds down. What little light oozes in is swallowed by heavy curtains on all sides, made of some kind of tangled material. The air is dusty and ancient, chemical and alien, fetid and organic at the same time. It is something quite unlike the air-conditioned and deodorised smell of the building.

Rhys becomes aware of a shape moving behind the curtain, the material stirs but he can't make it resolve into anything meaningful. Now a scratching sound rises all around, white noise that somehow becomes a voice, a voice without any clear source. It is matey RP, its tone chummy condolence, but those inhuman sounds and odours don't just underlie it they somehow seem to constitute it.

'Rhys. Good to talk at last. Name to a face. Sorry it has to be under these circumstances. Unauthorised absence. Serious matter. Tough times for everyone. Concerns. Dreadfully sorry to tell you this, mate.'

That vast dark shape swells closer to the curtain, pushing against the thick ropes of matted, twisted filth. The voice continues but that undertow of chattering, shrieking noises from all around now rises until only fragments of sense are discernible.

'Commitment. Time and motion. Skillset. Workflow. Competitive advantage. Thought leaders. Market makers. Did you see the match on Saturday? Human capital. Human resources. I've got kids myself. Evolve. Strive. Feed. Rebrand. Restructure. Regret. Never did me any harm.'

Rhys glimpses his own face reflected in a dark pool of an eye. Two eyes. Then four. Pressing through those dense, fetid rags of web. A shapeless moving, dripping cave of a mouth.

'Options exhausted. Regret. Lieu of notice. Evolve. Feed. Grow. Regards to the family. Pleasure. A question of attitude. Redundant. Sadly. Compete. Evolve. Strive. Feed. Grow. Regret. Regret. Regret.'

THE HOLLOW SHORE

Gary Budden

Julie left on Christmas Day. Married for three years, together for five. Upped and left with the gravy and roast potatoes still steaming on our clean new Ikea flooring, uneaten evidence of the final argument. What a waste of food.

I drank through Christmas and New Year, taking advantage of the offers on at the local Sainsbury's. I walked by my local library daily, saw its crumbling walls and raw wounds as machines began the demolition. Galliford Try signs apologised for any inconvenience and announced a new cultural centre, luxury apartments, a new café. Crane-necked metal beasts ripped out the building's innards and exposed them to dusty air. Sometimes I stopped and chatted with Tom, the loquacious local drunk who sat on a plastic chair opposite the ruins, offering boozy wisdom to passersby. 'They didn't listen,' is what he said most often.

Eventually a new year came and I returned to work. I filled my free time with books, movies, drink and the occasional line. I fumbled with a woman ten years my junior in the gents of a gastropub up Clapton, so new the toilet walls were free of graffiti and sexual innuendo. Life as it was rumbled on.

I sat at home listening to the records Julie never really liked, at wall shaking volume ignoring the bangs on walls from my neighbours. A pile of unopened envelopes grew on the kitchen table. This flat in east London, we'd signed the lease together, split the rent fifty-fifty, the energy bills, the Plusnet, everything. My job paid me a half-decent wage but I was going out more, missing a day of work here and there, using the credit card for everyday essentials. At night, when I finally fell asleep, I waded through waterlogged saltmarsh, mud-spattered and exhausted, running from a black-clad figure that sighed and moaned like the wind behind me. I woke with a splitting headache, hollowed-out, sweating, my tongue sandpaper dry and tasting of ash. I gulped cold water from the bathroom tap, splashed it over my face, stared at a reflection I didn't much care for. On insomniac nights I sat on the sofa we bought together from John Lewis, now stained with beer and smudged grey, watching films I'd downloaded illegally onto a hard-drive. Julie left me most of the stuff, the physical objects we purchased, the *things* we paid dearly for. Our accumulated life a list of brand names, furniture, gourmet coffee and organic veg boxes.

I watched English Civil War films, 70s ghost stories, Satanic rituals in England's ancient forests. I spent hours at the laptop drowning in pornography. Every morning a new arrears notice stared up from the doormat. Once, I tried to phone her, more out of duty than need. That's what people did in these situations. I heard she was living with a suit who worked in the City, in his flat in Canary Wharf and weekending at his place in Surrey. She never picked up. I was glad.

By the following winter it was all gone. I was let go when work downsized. I couldn't afford my rent. The credit card bills were piling up. I ignored calls from unknown numbers. Arrears on the water, electricity, gas. Plusnet cut me off. At least I still had the car.

The night before eviction, after a day of piling books and records into the boot, packing clothes and filling out change of address forms, I sat and drank from a good bottle of whisky, stared at my laptop, clicking on sites about the best walking routes in East Kent.

The next morning I posted the keys through the letterbox, got in the car and drove out through Homerton, under the Hackney Wick flyover through the Blackwall tunnel and onto the outskirts of Faversham.

That's how I ended up living with two ageing people I called my parents for the first time in seventeen years, in an old Victorian house that had been my childhood home, five minutes walk from Faversham Creek. As I drove, feeling London fall away behind me, my life boxed up in the boot, I felt happy for the first time in months.

*

Early Sunday afternoon, grey. Dad silent in the passenger seat, Mum in the back talking about a friend from work's son's wedding, seemingly to herself. I drove us down the Thanet Way, easing through a patch of floodwater from the recent rains, for Sunday lunch at a venue of their choosing. Harvester. Our first Sunday lunch since I left the city and the first as a trio in many years. I parked up. They went on ahead *to get a good spot* while I locked up. I paused, looking around the sparsely populated car-park, bleached crisp packets and fag butts. Felt the rain on my skin and listened to the traffic. A solitary crow watched me curiously, perched in a patch of polluted scrub. This wasn't how I remembered it.

I walked in through the glass doors into the anodyne warmth of the restaurant, ochre-red, an antiseptic womb. My mother waved from the good spot they'd secured. I scanned the dining area. Perhaps five other tables occupied. We were here early, *to beat the lunchtime rush.* A young black-haired waitress with a thick estuary accent and a painted smile led me to the table. She took our drinks order and laid down laminated menus as I pulled my seat out. Lager for me, coffee for my parents.

The waitress scurried off in the direction of the bar.

'So how's the job hunt going Simon?' my father asked, barely looking up from his *Telegraph*.

'Leave the boy alone he's had a tough year!' said Mum. 'He'll get round to it, won't you Simon?'

Mercifully, the conversation was delayed by the waitress arriving with the drinks. I grabbed mine and took a large gulp. A flash of that painted smile before she disappeared.

'He's 35 years old. Not a boy anymore,' grunted Dad as he reached for his coffee. FEARS OVER ROMA MIGRANTS INCREASE, the paper's headline.

I sighed and sipped my pint. 'I'm on it tomorrow. I've only been down a day. There's a recession on, you know. Let's enjoy our lunch together, can we? Come on, have a look and see what you want.'

Mum squinted at the menu, talking away to herself and firing questions at Dad about did he remember what he had last time, and did they still do those lovely fajita-things? I took a quick look, settled on the vegetarian lasagne. My parents took their time. I watched my fellow diners. At one table sat a silent septuagenarian couple poking forks into identical plates of mixed grill. At another, a young mother tried vainly to control the actions of her gurgling toddlers. Her boyfriend, husband perhaps, looked meek and tired and simply smiled as she dealt with the children. In the distance, the bar and service area, where young, white-shirted staff, none more than twenty years old, yawned and tried to look alert for potential customers. Over a weak set of speakers leaked commercial pop music, sugary declarations of love, auto-tuned broken hearts. On the walls hung bleak images of the Kent coast and marshlands; a beckoning black-clad figure distinct in a dwarfing landscape. Crashing waves hitting sandstone by Reculver towers. A portrait of a black curlew, hiding in the reeds. Figures not waving but drowning.

Only one picture I recognised, Dyce's *Pegwell Bay*. I'd seen it in the Tate, with Julie, a few years back. A Victorian family gathered shells, sifted through geological and chronological strata. Donati's comet, faintly visible, trailed through the sky. I told my wife about my trips to that same bay as a child, of the fake Viking ship and the hover-port, the shells I collected with Dad. I wondered who made the artistic decisions at Harvester.

'Simon?'

'Yes, mum?'

'I was saying, are you ready to order?'

'Yep, all decided.'

I swallowed the rest of my pint in three big gulps and beckoned the waitress over. I ordered another lager along with the food, paused, then asked. 'Dad, Mum, why didn't we go to one of the old pubs in Faversham? In Whitstable? There's loads of lovely old places round here with decent pub grub. Good ale. A bit of character. And you choose a Harvester by the Thanet Way?'

My father looked up from his paper. 'We like it here.' For the first time that day, he smiled.

*

I was setting up my stuff in my childhood room. A few Christmases back, Julie and I stayed in here, revelling in the quiet and the pitch-black night.

I ripped gaffa tape off a brown cardboard box that was weighing down the mattress. Old books and LPs, vinyl I'd carried on collecting long after selling all my CDs. I sat on the bed picking through my detritus. *Thunder and Consolation. Avocet. Borderline.* Julie said my taste in music was well out of touch. I liked it like that. I slung books onto the duvet, novels, travel writing, landscape poems, old copies of *Magnesium Burns* fanzine. I flicked through an illustrated guide to British birds, read a random entry on marsh harriers. I found a stash of bent photographs from years back, pictures of me and my mate Dave at a party up at The Balustrade in North London. Dave grinning with his wife-to-be Becky, me with my then-girlfriend Adrianna, her hair dyed, lip pierced, and now a crease splitting her from head to navel. The Balustrade got knocked down years back, replaced with flats and a franchise coffee shop. Memories trapped in cement, waiting to be discovered like sabre-toothed beasts in tar pits.

I carried on unpacking, found an old guidebook I must have bought nearly fifteen years ago. *Esoteric Kent: A Guide to the Hidden Walkways and Roads Less Travelled of the Garden of England.* I opened it up and looked at the publication date. 1998, The Malachite Press. Sixteen years ago. What had changed since then? Was the Thanet Way as busy, had the Harvester already appeared? As I flicked through the book, I came across writing scrawled in blue ink on the title page. *Happy 19th birthday, all the love in the world. Mum & Dad xxx.* I sat on the bed, just holding the book, for a long time.

Only three days here. Housing developments grew in the corner of my eye, concrete putting down underground tendrils like fungus and potentially just as poisonous. More roads, more cars. In the local papers there was talk of airports in the Thames Estuary, an expansion for the airport at Lydd near Dungeness. I thought of Tom and wondered if he still kept his vigil by the disintegrating library.
Tomorrow morning I was signing on. I decided to do a bit of walking, out from my parents', a long walk through Faversham Creek along the Hollow Shore and onto the pubs of Whitstable. Take a few photographs, get some salty air in my lungs, recalibrate myself. Maybe at the weekend.

That night I sat in my reclaimed room and listened to a few punked-up folk songs on my stereo at low volume. The pictures of The Balustrade had stirred something up. I sent a text to Dave to see if he fancied coming down.

I wondered what Adrianna was doing now. I heard she moved back to Kent. I drank a few bottles of cider, *Esoteric Kent* open beside me, and searched for her online. There she was, so easy to find. Lives in **Faversham, Kent**. From **Faversham, Kent**. I said *fuck it* aloud, and sent the message.

*

Signing on was miserable. Going through my CV, a hollow list of achievements, being told what I already knew, that there were no jobs fitting what I was looking for round here. *I'll be looking for work in London, I'm just staying awhile with my parents* didn't seem to register. *Even if you wanted a job stacking shelves in Sainsbury's, which there aren't, you wouldn't get it, because you're overqualified.*

Relieved to be out, I walked into Faversham town centre. It was still early. A few gulls in winter plumage perched on the rooftops. I sat on a bench in front of The Black Curlew pub, looking at the old town hall, smoking a cigarette and eating a vegetable pasty bought from a franchise bakery. I watched people shuffle around the town.

Dave had agreed to come down on Friday. The plan was a couple of pints in The White Fox, then up early the next morning, to walk the Hollow Shore from Faversham to Whitstable. Dave was one of my oldest friends. It was through him I met Julie. They still kept in touch, I heard.

On the other side of the square sat a man in frayed black clothing and heavy workboots, head down and features obscured. He clutched a Tesco bag, smoking a rollup. The word *grizzled* came to mind. He looked like the photographs of men who once worked the shores and creeks of this county, those photographs that stood next to snippets of text on sun-faded and water-damaged information signs, next to spots of historical interest. He barely moved, seemed superimposed, like he'd been badly Photoshopped in.

I watched him awhile before heading back.

*

My parents were out at work. It was nearly midday. I sat on their new sofa they'd recently bought at DFS with the giant flat-screen HD TV playing muted re-runs of *Homes Under the Hammer.* I had the laptop open, with tabs and tabs of recruitment sites jostling for pole-position. Already tired by the job hunt, I picked up my copy of *Esoteric Kent* and looked for the entry on the Hollow Shore:

A particularly good stretch is the marshy coast from Faversham to Whitstable (9.8 miles). It is entirely flat and fairly easy to navigate. Starting at the market square in the pretty medieval town of Faversham, you walk along historic Court Street, which becomes Abbey Street, and then joins the Saxon Shore Way. The walk takes you along creek and shoreline, across fields and past nature reserves, home to a rare breeding colony of black curlew. Eventually Whitstable appears, as does the Old Neptune pub, the perfect place to stop for a pint, before continuing on to tiny Wheeler's Oyster Bar for a seafood feast.

Esoteric facts: As part of the Saxon Shoreway, the Hollow Shore has been the site of numerous ghost sightings over the years with records of an unidentified black-clad figure being spotted out in the reed beds, dating back to the early nineteenth century. A number of sightings from the 1960s also claimed that the semi-mythic white foxes of Kent have been seen along the Hollow Shore, but at time of writing these claims are still unsubstantiated.

I closed the book, clicking my tongue in thought.

On the mantelpiece still stood a photograph of Julie and me on our wedding day, all polished grins and expensive clothing. Julie said I looked like I was due for a day in court when in my suit. I laughed at the memory. I got up and put the photo face down on the mantel. I resumed my job hunt, got distracted, checked my messages. New message, from Adrianna. In her profile picture, she'd let her hair revert back to its natural nut brown. The pierced lip remained. She held a small child in her arms.

Hi Simon, thanks for getting in touch!
Can't believe you're back in Kent! You always said you couldn't wait to get away from the place! I heard about you and Julie, so sorry. I'm still in touch with Dave, he told me what happened.

Thought about contacting you. Should have. I'm bad at staying in touch.
Shall we meet for a coffee? My number is _____

Xxx Ade

I replied and arrangements were made.

*

Thursday. Adrianna sat opposite me, steam in the air, coffee machines rumbling and hissing behind the counter. She hadn't brought Jenny, her daughter. 'She's with her dad in Canterbury', she explained. We were in The Linnet, a tiny café, busy this lunchtime. I looked at the woman in front of me and thought of a girl with purple hair and a crease running from head to navel. She looked so different, utterly familiar.

'So how you doing?'

'I've had better years, put it that way. It's good to see you Ade. You know, I found some photos of all of us, up at The Balustrade if you remember it. That's why I got in touch, really.'

'Because of some photos?' She laughed and sipped her coffee. 'Of course I remember it. Long gone now right?'

I nodded, tried to explain.

'No, I mean…I don't know. I saw that you were back living here. I guess I realised how long it had been. How did you end up back living here then?'

She talked for a long time interrupted, winter sun glinting off her lip, explaining how she'd met a guy after me, Danny, how they hit it off in London and spent a good few years drinking and dancing in the grotty venues of New Cross and Hackney ('Before all the coffee shops!') I knew bits of this story but didn't interrupt. Jenny was never planned, but at the time Adrianna and Danny were in love and the pieces felt like they were falling into place. Cheaper to move out of the city, they decided. Danny was from Essex, near Canvey Island, but he didn't mind the idea of Kent. They settled in Canterbury. A good place for kids, she said – 'Well we both know that, don't we?' – and I said yes, but possibly a bad one for teenagers. She laughed at that. Jenny was born, things were OK for a bit, then it all broke down, not for any real reason, they were still amicable but it just wasn't working any more.

'Same with me and Julie, really.'

She nodded. 'So what's it like being back here then?'

'My mother, bless her, drives me up the wall. I need to find work. I should probably be in a worse mood than I am. I'm liking the peace and quiet, planning on do a bit of walking, that kind of thing.'

'You realise how noisy and stressful London is right? Maybe I'll come with you on one of these walks.'

'That'd be nice. I've got Dave coming down tomorrow, but I'd love to arrange something soon. You can bring Jenny if you like.'

She smiled at that and drained her coffee.

*

Friday. I picked Dave up from Faversham station. I didn't really need to drive and he knew the way to my parents' place, he'd been there innumerable times as a teenager, the two of us smoking weed out the window in my upstairs bedroom, downloading pictures of topless women on the creaky internet we had back in '98. But driving was what adults did.

As I pulled up to the station he was already outside, shivering slightly and looking up and down the street. He probably hadn't been to this town in fifteen years. Behind him, a billboard poster advertised a new installation up at The Gallery in Margate, named merely 'The Exhibition' by artist Helena Williams. Her name sounded familiar. I squinted to read the title of the image they'd picked for this advert. '*Cinque or Swim*', *Helena Williams, 2009.*

I honked the horn. Dave spotted me and climbed into the passenger seat.

'Easy mate, how's things?' We shook hands.

'Not too bad, considering.'

'This place aint changed much has it?'

'I dunno. Yes and no. There's more people but it feels almost quieter than when I left.'

'No mean feat!' He grinned.

We dumped Dave's stuff back at the house, made a bit of small talk with my parents who asked about Dave's parents, about his son and his ex-wife Becky, how life was up in Lewisham, before we set off on foot out into the Faversham Friday night.

It seemed quiet. Perhaps it had always been like this, when we tried our luck in the pubs as boys. We walked into town back past the station, a group of girls in their late-teens trembling in the cold, pulling inadequate jackets over themselves in a futile attempt to keep warm. Walked onto the market square, The Black Curlew slowly filling with punters. Dodged a middle-aged woman clearly already worse for wear, laying into an exasperated friend, then down a little side alley and through the swimming pool car park onto The White Fox, a decent pub that had been a favourite of ours back in the day.

Dave flung a spent cigarette on the floor as we approached. 'God I haven't been here in years. Good to be back, actually.'

I nodded.

We entered, the light reassuringly dim. The place still felt like a pub. A place to drink, with a friend. Little from what I could see, bar the free Wifi, had changed in the last fifteen years. Maybe a bit cleaner. The faint smell of disinfectant and piss that all pubs now had, post smoking ban. Like all the pubs round here, it was Shepherd Neame. I ordered two pints of Whitstable Bay while Dave found a seat. The pub was busy but not yet crowded, a few lads either side of the cusp of drinking age furtively sipping cider, a couple of old men in thick jumpers at the bar who stared at nothing in particular, a couple in their thirties with a bottle of red. The barmaid flashed a painted smile as she handed over the pints. On the bar's smooth polished surface were a few cardboard fliers for 'The Exhibition', sticky with evaporated beer.

Dave had found a decent spot in the corner. It was good to see him. We spent the evening sinking pints, both of us now single, a thought unimaginable when we'd celebrated and laughed *your life's over* at each other's weddings, popping champagne corks, eating expensive canapés and kissing the women who were then our future. He talked about his son and how he missed him, feared for the world he was inheriting, this brandscape that was shutting down any possibility. I talked about my parents and their choice of restaurants, of airport expansions, of Tom and the library, of Julie and our trips to Ikea, John Lewis and Waitrose. We planned our walk along the Hollow Shore from this town to Whitstable, said we shouldn't drink too much we've got an early start, a plan we didn't stick to. The pub filled. Teenage girls sank shots of lurid liquids. Old men mumbled, drank everlasting pints. A fight began between alcohol-pink aftershaved boys, spilling out the door and into the car park with jeers and hoots. Dave laughed, slapped me on the back, cried, 'See some things round here never change!'

*

We woke early, just before dawn, rubbing nicotine stained fingers over greying stubble, stumbled to the bathroom for a quick wash, to scrub the sugar and alcohol from our yellowing teeth. I pulled my walking boots on in an early-morning haze. I remembered when I bought them, with Julie, cheap and on offer from our local Sports Direct. *How come there are so many of these places?* she asked once. *They breed like rabbits.* Dave and I clumped down the stairs to find Mum already awake, dressed, brewing a pot of strong coffee, and in that moment, all the times she'd been at that same counter on any cold morning like this, making breakfast for Dad, packing my sister's lunchbox in the 90s, making me some porridge, all came back and I felt guilt and raw nostalgia, I wondered what her life had been like, had it really turned out the way she'd wanted and why did I give her a hard time about Harvesters and her interminable anecdotes? *I'm sorry, Mum, for everything.* The words ran through my head on loop, failed to form themselves on my lips.

Dave gratefully took a large cup of coffee. I did the same, my mug showing an artist's sketch of a black curlew. *Ta mum!* I said grinning, wrapping my arm round her shoulder. She was so small. She was happy I was here, I realised.

I packed *Esoteric Kent* into my backpack with something for lunch, a bit of fruit, bottles of water. The walk was only nine miles and we aimed to end up at The Old Neptune in Whitstable by early afternoon for more pints and a decent lunch. We set off, walking into a morning weighed down with mist, through deserted streets onto Faversham Creek, past sleeping restaurants and artisan shops, into the realms of the boat people, a few of whom were already up and active, wraith-like in the mist chopping logs and wrapped in dew soaked fleeces. A woman looked up silently from her chopping as we passed, axe in hand, standing in front of a mildewed boat named *Reynardine.* The mist was a thick, wet swaddling. Boats bobbed on the waters of the creek, the tide low, carved mudflats becoming visible. Turnstones flitted about, gliding in small groups over the creek. I heard the cry of a black curlew somewhere far out on the saltmarsh.

Dave ducked his head as he walked under a large houseboat, *Jack Orion,* propped up on lichened and mossy wooden poles, groaning and creaking like the old men in The White Fox. We came to the end of the boat people's territory, pushed through a squeaking gate, splashed muddy through puddles that dotted the path to the Hollow Shore like some inverted miniature archipelago.

We came to what once must have been a winch for unloading and loading goods, in those hazy days of proud British maritime history. Now rust patches like orange fungus burst through the flaking white paint, and a hook swung gently on frayed rope. A metallic gallows that stood guard to a rickety wooden bridge crossing the creek. We crossed, looking down the impossible distances to the mudflats where I saw sandpipers dart and dash, and then we were onto the saltmarsh.

We walked and we talked, talked about everything from our childhoods to the abandoned psychiatric hospital rumoured to be rotting out in the Kent countryside, of environmental therapies, the music and books we loved, old memories and fresh stories, the healing effects of horticulture and the debate of town versus city. I told him that I'd met up with Adrianna, and he grinned, but shook his head.

'Do you really want to open old wounds?'

I thought for a moment, and said, 'Yeah, I think I do'.

The path was still sodden from the recent rains, my boots slick with creamy mud, the wind off the Swale increasing its ferocity. This landscape, so flat, barren and beautiful. Icy wind formed tears in my eyes. I paused and leaned against an Environment Agency sign, a litany of danger spelled out in yellow and black; drowning, floods, electrocution. The violence out here easy to imagine.

'Come look at this!' Dave beckoned me over to the concrete wall separating the grassy path from the shore. Bladderwrack carpeted the shoreline before giving way to low-tide mudflats. Over the water, the Isle of Sheppey so close it felt like it was within touching distance. I thought of the prisons there, that solitary bridge connecting the island to the mainland, and the boxing hares I'd watched with Dad when I was nine years old. I saw a black clad figure on the opposite shoreline, waving.

Dave pointed at a small boat that was half submerged in the eager mud, it's prow buried like it was rooting for lugworms. The rust and decay, the ruins and the mildewed boats, these forgotten paths, were too good not to record. He hopped onto the shingle and edged towards it. I watched him clamber and slip on deep-green seaweed as he approached the boat, camera snapping away, spattered mud forming abstract patterns on his jeans. Who would ever have thought the two of us would still be here, in the place where we grew up, post-marriage, muddy as fuck, taking pictures of rusty boats on our smartphones.

I was glad we were still mates. Marriage didn't make me happy. Didn't make her happy either. I was happier here than I'd been in ages, dirty, cold and wet.

Even the pylons looked beautiful.

I lit a cigarette, watching Dave slip and slide on the bladderwrack. A group of cormorants flapped overhead. I listened to the sigh of the marshes.

The walk continued for aeons, two lone figures the only ones privy to the giant suspended sky, the shining shingle, the discovery of space in this most crowded of counties. Dave, keen-eyed for ruin, spotted another wreckage, some unidentifiable amalgam of rusted machinery slipping into the marsh, hungry plant life colonising the metal.

'Something they used when people still worked for a living!', he said sourly, before hopping off the path and wading through foot-high reeds to get a better view, smartphone held tight. I heard a wet sucking sound. Dave disappeared from view. I threw my smouldering cigarette butt into a mud pool, shouted my friends' name again and again. Panic, a thumping heart, cold beads of sweat breaking on my forehead. I tried to calm myself, fumbled for my phone to call someone, anyone. No reception.

An ash-white animal trotted onto the path in front of me, yellow eyes gleaming, its head splitting into a huge canine yawn. It watched me curiously. Further along the path a black-clad figure in heavy, muddy work boots stood clutching a Tesco bag close to his chest, smoke from his cigarette forming a nimbus around his obscured features. He beckoned towards the reeds. I thought of Julie and roast potatoes cooling on Ikea flooring, my parents silent in a womb-red Harvester, painted smiles, Tom downing a can of Special Brew as the library crumbled, Dave eyeing up the girls in The White Fox, Adrianna creased from head to navel, black curlews nesting in the reeds, concrete roots pushing deeper and deeper down into the soil, an estuary covered in tarmac, a world of endless flats and cafés.

I walked towards him, the white fox following at my heels, hollow and at peace.

CHINESE PYGMALION

Elaine Chiew

This bread has eczema. This cousin of mine eyes the farmhouse white bread dusted with flour, rubs a finger over the white dust and applies it like lipstick on her lips. Elly's been here four days. Actions have consequences; there's a logical progression to things. Elly bunks with me. She's in my face. I rough it out in a Bivy sack. My MSN Messenger pings with chat windows. Orgasm Addict, Terra Vagina, Pop Vanguardist, Tranvestite Villain – London is calling. I hear a wall of noise. An amphetamine of screeches and caterwauls. Elly gazes at me with the solemnity of a dead penguin.

Her mother tried to gas herself in a car in her garage. Babysit Elly, Mum says. How long will she be here? In response, she threatens to take away my allowance. Elly's world is one of free association. Bomb is a four-letter word. Don't use that word with me, young man. Fuck is a four-letter word. So is cunt. I'm grounded for a week.

Our Chelsea mews house does not have a guest room. Elly's hands are forever in my things. She sniffs and scratches my clothes. If she touches my computer, she's dead meat.

When my computer screen pings, she turns her face away. I've made a new friend in an internet chatroom – he calls himself Chinese Pygmalion. He has flawed views. Chinese Pygmalion says there's a lack of musical ideas – bands produce these padded tracks, repetitive, bland, monochromatic – if you've heard one Oasis, you've heard them all. Elly says music gives her mountain pectorals. She says she hates music. She jerks her head back and forth like an ostrich.

I bury myself under earphones. Now there's a banging in my head – the rush of a music jam – thrumming, stopping, starting, glutinous electric slides, a total enmeshment of leftover arpeggios, psychedelic dream remnants and drenched lyricism. Like Chinese food acid reflux. I think of Chinese Pygmalion's grand music theories.

A new chat window pops up on my computer screen.

[Chinese Pygmalion]: didya listen to The Slits like I recommended?
[Simon Coco-Muncher]: no, just Matchbox 20 and Smashing Pumpkins.
[Chinese Pygmalion]: Fucking gormless jabbered harmonies. Pathetic shit.
[Simon Coco-Muncher]: Am I in the wrong generation?
[Chinese Pygmalion]: It's all cagoules, day-glo effects and fishtail parkas for you lot.
[Simon Coco-Muncher]: Don't plex me. I don't give a toss about Gwen Stefani either.
[Chinese Pygmalion]: Oh, chill.
[Chinese Pygmalion]: Didya send your pix yet? Shall we meet?
[Chinese Pygmalion]: How old are you?
[Simon Coco-Muncher]: I'm not telling.

I think he's lying about his age. He tells me he's thirty-two, lives in Camden Town. He tells me he watched The Pop Group at a rally off Trafalgar Square as a teenager. I google that. A rally to protest the use of Britain as an American missile launch pad.

Elly stares at me with the eyes of a waterfowl. She jerks her head back and forth like an ostrich. She wanders the hallways of our house. I hear her knocking softly along the walls. I google Chinese Pygmalion. I google his information. October 1980: there was a rally off Trafalgar Square featuring The Pop Group. Chinese Pygmalion is a liar. He must be close to fifty. But why? Why lie about your age?

Elly is nine. I'm fifteen. Safety pins, rat-traps, swastikas. When Chinese Pygmalion was in his teens, he wore these things. He told me. Elly wears a crocheted top. It has a large ugly flower pinned to its lapel. The flower looks like a Venus fly-trap. Venus fly-traps can swallow a whole small furry animal. When Elly was five, she was massively fat. Her skin harboured a rash that snaked and flowered when she was flustered. Elly watches me like a cyclop, covering one eye. She's fucking weird. She watches me all day long.

Don't you think it's inappropriate for a young male teen to be in a room with a young girl? Mum's eyes bulge at this attempt of mine to evict Elly. When Mum's eyes bulge, I know I'm in carpetbombing territory. Before your Aunt Polly tried to kill herself, Mum says, very quietly, she had several miscarriages. And one baby was born and only lived for a week.

I could recount history too. Before Aunt Polly tried to kill herself, Mum and Aunt Polly had these conversations.

Aunt Polly: Is there something wrong with Simon's voice? You should get his voicebox checked. Could be a hormonal problem. I mean, he is beyond that delicate age of puberty, isn't he?
Mum: Simon is sensitive. There's nothing wrong with sensitive.
Aunt Polly: He's not sensitive. I wouldn't call it sensitive. Are you sure he's not…you know?
Mum: What? What are you trying to say?
Aunt Polly: You didn't care about organic. You thought I was going overboard. Well, did you know eating hormonally injected cows and drinking their milk make young boys grow

tits and turn them into poncy fruitcakes?
Mum: What are you talking about? I can't understand you.
Aunt Polly: Do you really not understand or do you just choose
not to see?

*

So there you are. Poor Elly. Her mother tried to gas herself.
Her father ran off with the tarty neighbour from upstairs
who owns a cat and fancy galoshes and flirts with the leaf-
blower man while she parks her car too far from the kerb. Elly
whispers shiso-shiso-shiso along the corridors. She watches me
sleep at night with owl-eyes. She stares at her eggs for breakfast
and says that the yolks are trembling with fear. Music gives her
mountain pectorals and marmalade is a place of alien skid.

Elly has broken lyricism. That's how Chinese Pygmalion
explains it. It's a common disease among freaks and miscreants.
Elly eats a spoonful of yogurt speckled with fresh raspberries. She
says that the Queen's beefeaters are swimming in the Thames.

[Chinese Pygmalion]: Shall we meet? He puts a smiley face
with heart shapes for eyes. Then, when I don't answer, he sends
me a picture of his cock. It is large, with corrugated folds,
a dark shade of purple. I enlarge the picture. It is no longer
identifiable. Elly watches me like a cyclop. I stuff the picture
with me in my Bivy sack.

*

Lurid dreams. Simon CocoMuncher has lurid dreams.
He plays the EML 200 synth. The bass glistens wetly.
The drummer shakes his shaggy mane. The lead vocalist is
Chinese. He screeches through his reedy voicebox. We play
roundelays that breach barriers between politics and poetry,
lust and spirituality. In our dreams, the music crescendoes are
a maelstrom of writhing noise and pop extravaganza. The lead

vocalist grabs his cock. The bass player strips off his T-shirt and trousers. He is naked. He turns around and tugs Simon on the arm.

In the dark, a girlish voice whispers. Are you hurt, Simon? I wake up. Elly's face is very close. As round as the moon, it hovers like a wheel of cheese. You were screaming.

I was singing, thank you very much.

Your screams are gridzones of anomie.

*

We fetch up outside the bus-stand. I've got Ipod nubs in my ears. The energetic slide of ZZ Top's *Legs*. Chinese Pygmalion recommends ZZ Top. I'm working through a playlist of his recommendations. Joy Division. Cabaret Voltaire. Throbbing Gristle. Violent Femmes. Buzzcocks. Siouxsie and The Banshees. These bands set the music panorama afire with new sonic expressionism and their peripatetic embrace of electronics, noise, reggae dub techniques, disco production! Chinese Pygmalion lives in an alternate reality. His picture gives me a violent, dangerous thrill.

Chinese Pygmalion is looking for a Brian Eno-type to produce his music, to spot his star rising on the ascendancy.

[Chinese Pygmalion]: Okey dokey, what will it be? We will meet in Camden Town.

Café culture, reggae roots, the zis-boom-bah of the music club scene. It could be dangerous. Then again, it could be exciting. I'm fifteen. Elly is nine. What will I do with Elly?

*

Elly looks up the road. No. 22 is rumbling towards us. A lady is pushing a baby carriage through the puffin crossing. Two teenagers follow on her heels. One wears a trilby and a long coat. The other wears a cagoule and low-slung baggy jeans. He shuffles-shuffles. Elly whispers shiso-shiso. *April Skies* thrum-thrum in my ears.

No. 19 is right snug behind 22. We wave it down. Elly counts out exact fare. The bus driver stares. His sclera glows white. An old lady in a babushka behind us taps her cane. I rock side to side. Elly does the ostrich shuffle. In the bus, her finger hovers over the red push button while the other hand slides up and down the yellow pole. Suddenly, it makes sense. Elly doesn't hate music. She holds my hand as we sway on the bus.

We are hungry. We get off on Picadilly right in front of the parabolic track of a side-winding scooter. It misses her by inches. If Elly screams, the screen will freeze with moisture drops caught in pearly stationary pose like glittering meth crystals. The acid roar in my ears is rage. *Sometimes* by My Bloody Valentine. The electro-juddering guitar, the elliptical detached vocals of Kevin Shields – what a master of tone controls! – the words 'Turn my head, into sound…' giving me an eerie spine-jingle. It's the world of scene shifting around me, a sliding periscope. Elly is shaking. Her eyes are enlarged, violet with fright. Her face dips. The furze of golden down on the profile of her face is raised as hackles.

Dying is just a metallic snap, she says.

It can happen, I say.

The Japan Centre slides into view. We troop inside with the promise of a bowl of udon for under ten quid a piece. My head is ringing. *Heaven* by the Cocteau Twins. Chinese Pygmalion is waiting in Camden Town.

*

She twists and turns on her stool. Then, she pulls the nubs out of my ears.

Why do you tune people out? Her feet skid up and down the board below the counter, the beat percussive.

We wait for udon. Udon mania in here. Chilled soba. Nabeyaki udon. Sanuki udon. Harusame noodles and fish tempura. Elly grins. Her sclera glows white. Live tentacles, tangled in skeins, ziggurats of worms. My fist closes around her upper arm.

Elly squirms in pain. I know you hate me, Simon, but I'm the only one who can save you. Her smile is coquettish. She's kitted out in a green tartan skirt, purple tights, a flea-bitten jumper of *101 Dalmations*. On her head, an Alice hairband that looks like a Christmas wreath, on her feet, ballet pumps with a zebra print, and on her wrists, friendship beads, Indian bangles, a charm bracelet.

She smears the broth of her sanuki udon all over her lips and cheeks. She whispers. Glossy tallow. And again. Glossy tallow. Her eyes are mean little slits.

A guerrilla-red wall of chewed-up noodles and broth shoots up my nostrils.

Have you been peeking at my mail? I sputter. I choke and spit out goo. Chinese Pygmalion wrote about Devo's sex songs. Mothersbaugh imagines female secretions smeared all over him like glossy tallow.

Come smear all over me. Come smear all over me. She mimics, intoning something she's read of mine. Again, that nasty, mean little grin. Her eyes dance like live wire. She's just like Aunt Polly.

I take a deep breath. I take another. In the space of two beats, something comes to me. Vic Goddard, the lead singer of Subway Sect was as unrock-and-roll as you could get, preferring to conduct interviews in ice-cream parlours rather than pubs. He talked about bird-watching and golf. Later, he became a postman. The unapologetic baleful ugliness of the corpulent and gnarly Dave Thomas of Pere Ubu was an affront and a statement. PiL's personal zeitgeist was total control of its public image, down to Wobble sporting his 1920s lounge-lizard moustache. They were Epicenters of a Quake Compressed. My new heroes. Heroes I learned about through Chinese Pygmalion.

Dizzy waves of heat spiral and scratch to and fro on my spine. My hand rises up, unpremeditated, then descends. It makes a resounding connect that leaves a hand print on her cheek like a flowering Venus flytrap. Elly bursts like a plastic bag of air and moisture. Big, fat drops splashing into her sanuki udon. I throw two tenners on the wooden counter. My hakata ramen unfinished. Ziggurats of worm. Elly's poison smears over everything, the spread of purple squid ink, the seep of invisible molecules of carbon monoxide, the spongy rise of foam-addled dreams, the psychedelic bleed of echo-and-reverb into cluster chords.

You're fucking Darfur in one slide, a walking disaster in one frame.

I can't be cool like you, Simon! She shouts. I do not flinch. Very deliberately, I leave her there.

*

I didn't expect the beret, the lounge-lizard moustache, the Crombie coat. I didn't expect the lumpen midriff roll, the tinted crenellated skin, the shrill, slightly sour warble, the dark purple sacs under his eyes. I didn't expect that he was not Chinese at all.

Pygmalion is one of the most original album of the shoegazing movement. It's by Slowdive, and it's a worthwhile progression away from their pedal-laden indie beginnings towards a more mature, spacey and psychedelic style. But it's not an all-time classic. There's a lack of musical ideas – a repetitive, padded feeling to the tracks. He explains all this, and when he speaks, his moustache twitches. His eyes are electric blue, and the gaze slow and steady. His eyes roll up and down my frame. He keeps asking if I'm all right.

The noshery we pitched up at is several doors down from Dingwalls, in a farrago of cobble-stoned alleys off Chalk Farm Road overlooking the canal. The denizens of Camden Town are rappers, hip-hoppers, rock-and-rollers, cartoon punks, beat boys, fly girls. They are black velvet-caped goths reeking of ylang ylang. They are army surplus fused with Vivienne Westwood, sporting asymmetric haircuts. They are vaudeville and disguise. They are androgynous ghosts in pancake make-up.

Where's your cousin?

I don't answer. There is an unusually loud percussive beat about the place. A poster of the Sex Pistols on their *Filthy Lucre* tour in 1996 in Japan is immaculately framed. Also, there's a framed T-shirt with a snippet of dialogue from the Bill Grundy-Sex Pistols live broadcast interview on Thames Television, 1976. Plaster-of-Paris plaques tell me all these things.

A trail of water droplets leads to the gents. A subliminal undertow of unease in my gallstone and on this black noisescape. Chinese Pygmalion is a fount of wisdom and history: in music, rebellion is co-opted into mainstream commercialism. Take punk. Take any of the bands rising out of the ashes of punk. Take New Wave. Being bought out by the big outfits. Fame corrupts absolutely. The 80s' music was replete with incidences of style triumphing over content. The fatboy excess of the '80s has lead to the deadening of creative musical impulses. There are no grand musical theories, the way Eno used to espouse. There is banality. Coldplay, Travis, Snow Patrol, Take That, Plain White T's, Green Day. Cute melody jingles, lull strumming of guitars, mindless love-gone-bad lyrics. Pretty boy lead vocalists. Where's the samizdat culture of do-it-yourself – bands releasing their own records, local promoters organising gigs, independent labels with a philosophy of anti-corporate economics with a healthy smidgeon of left-wing politics? Ever heard of Fast Product?

Chinese Pygmalion explains how it was an arty label from the late '70s, how they inserted rotting orange peels and spliced collage pictures of German terrorists together with The Quality of Life album. Each peel would rot in a different way, making each copy of the EP unique, never to be duplicated. His sclera glows white. I gaze at his shoes. They are besmirched, with the heel of one boot coming ungummed.

Chinese Pygmalion's arms constantly chop the air, twanging a rhetorical guitar. He reaches into his pockets. The sound of granola-crunching in his pockets. Out comes a bag of pistachios and a homespun CD.

For you. Old but shweet.

He's got Iggy and the Stooges and Primal Scream and Velvet Underground and Manic Street Preachers on there. I stop reading. The earnest education of Simon Coco-Muncher. Chinese Pygmalion smiles. But the smile doesn't reach his eyes. And his tone is ironic. His teeth is as crooked as a set of graveyard tombstones. I don't mean to tell him about Elly, about leaving her. I don't mean to talk about rage. I don't mean to grind my lips together. I don't mean to demonstrate the wah-wah of the wall of noise banging in my skull. He listens, intent. A mild jangle of alarm, like adrenaline overdrive, kickstarts through my intestines. Chinese Pygmalion lifts his beret. His mashed hair is thinning, revealing a galaxy cluster of freckles on the pale limpid skin. A caul of untinctured skin at odds with the rest of him, the waterfall conjugations and strident theories, the carefully-constructed schmaltz.

She knows how to get home by herself?

I shake my head.

But she's a smart girl, yes? She'll sort herself out. You left her money?

What's left of it after the bill.

He nods. She's a bright girl, she'll work it out.

We sit for awhile. He doesn't say anything. He orders a Schlitz. The owner exchanges some sort of signal with him. My place isn't far from here. If you want, I can show you my album collection. He says this casually. His hand stretches out, briefly skims mine.

There's an incipient roar in my head now. A wired, plangent ringing of chords, an epic fat-bass riff of fitful disquiet.

We all do some bad things sometimes. It doesn't make us a bad person. He glances at the owner as he says this. The owner tilts his jaw. His eyes glitter from behind the metallic frames, watching me like a sniper.

You wanta come back and check out my place? His eyes are glowing like live black coals, the sclera egg-white.

I don't think I should, I say.

His fingers curl the air. I see talons. Over at the bar, the owner nods once. Chinese Pygmalion changes the subject, starts talking about his name, Pygmalion. Pygmalion is the myth of the artist in love with his subject, right? His obsession transforms the subject into live flesh. Pygmalion is also George Bernard Shaw's play. It's also *My Fair Lady*. Higgins turns Eliza Doolittle into a proper-enunciating tetchy little wench. Pygmalion is a bildungsroman. Know what a bildungsroman is?

Are you on something? Simon CocoMuncher sits on his hands and has a bad feeling.

He smiles again. Flash of graveyard tombstones. Pete. My real name's Pete. I don't tell everybody that, only very special people. I've got a feeling you're really special, Simon Coco-Muncher. His eyes hold a spectral glitter.

This could be your bildungsroman, Eliza Doolittle. He curls the air with his fingers. He winks. The afternoon is getting on, he whispers. He asks for the bill. When we stroll up to the till, the owner grips Chinese Pygmalion's fist in his own, shakes it and spits on it. Chinese Pygmalion looks as if he's in pain.

The owner turns to me. Don't ever trust this man.

*

We are outside in the warren of alleys. It is obscure; the sun does not reach it. It is shady and smells of stale beer and piss. He leans over. His lip-clamp on mine is a metallic grind of jowl and gristle, the fleshy bite of bicuspids, and the ashy taste of cigarettes.

He looks surprised when I shove my palm in his face.

It's what you wanted, isn't it?

You dirty fucker.

What a clever boy.

What a fucking rotter.
The taste of him is revolting.

*

He follows me on the Northern Line to Leicester Square. Ipod nubs in my ears, The Killers thumping a reverberation in my basal ganglia. I dodge, wend, swerve erratically, trying to give him the slip in the crowd. He's hot on my heels. He doesn't surrender easily. Catapulting like a limp rocket out of the underground, I spot a policeman on the beat mumbling into his walkie-talkie.

There's someone following me, sir!

The policeman glances where I'm pointing.

Chinese Pygmalion melts into the looming swathes of humanity, and is gone.

*

Back in the Japan Centre. The stool spins slowly with absence. Panic. Where is she?

She's endured my musical odysseys with eye cocked and the silence of a deer-hunter. She has sat, fists clenched, tension entrenched, through the meteoric crescendos of Led Zeppelin, Deep Purple and Nirvana. Teeth biting lower lip through the barrage of high-octane guitars of Buzzcocks and Throbbing Gristle.

I lay new tracks. Eagle Place, Jermyn Street, Maes Street, St James' Square. My heart thumps along with the base. I have to find her. There are a million possible scenarios. Kidnapping, robbery, run over by mopeds, mown down by pedestrians, entrapment, seduction, molestation. Trawl down Duke of York and Ormond Yard. Cramming, pushing, jostling through the Burlington Arcade, and to Old Bond. A body skittering, rotating through, clawing my way through a million possible permutations like bicycle spokes. Spinning as far as Conduit

Street, Great Marlborough Street, down the trout-packed crush of Carnaby shopping. Looking for a green tartan skirt and flea-bitten jumper with spotty dogs. A million 'if…then' algorithms spinning into infinities. I never meant to hurt her. I was just angry. Careening down Oxford Street, Wardour Street, Berwick, Lexington, Windmill, Picadilly Circus. A million dendrites of fear and despair. If I could depress a button and sift through the million worlds in this jukebox of life and order up a track, call it reality.

Exhausted now. In a total funk of agony and inconsolable distress. The façade of the Japan Center tips back and forth. In the gloaming, everything is ashen grey. In the gloaming, there's the claustrophobic certainty that something very bad has happened to Elly. Just as it did to Aunt Polly. There's no going back. Orange peels. Mum will have my skin, peel by peel. The thought of udon beckons. I am hungry and in need of comfort.

The hours creep past. I don't know what I'm waiting for. The noodles sit in my stomach like sour grease. My cell is constantly ringing. The panel lights up. It's Mum. There is no reason I can come up with for ditching Elly, none that would placate my mother. Then, through the bottom half of the double glass doors, I see a tartan skirt and a jumper with canine logo.

Elly!

It is and isn't her. A violent rash blooms through the skeletal white of her skin, and her eyes are dry and large and hollow. Something permanent has etched itself across her profile, leaving a bold signature. A smudge of dirt and a hand had left tracks on her neck.

Where the fuck have you been. I grab her by the shoulders.

I knew you'd come back for me, Simon. I knew you would. Her voice is tin-whistly, shrill.

Why? Why didn't you just wait for me then?

To punish you. She hisses. Her eyes glow with a sudden hot ember. An ember of hate. You're a big mean woolly gryffinch.

I'm sorry. I'm…Let's rip it up, start again.

She shakes her head. No chance. But it doesn't sound like she means it.

Come on, let me take you home.

I'm going to tell your mother. She sniffles. She blows her nose theatrically as we head towards the tube station. I trusted you, Simon. Elly says this, but almost to herself.

*

In the jolting train, we sit side by side on the padded seats. I take hold of Elly's small hand, burning hot and sweaty in mine. I squeeze and press, and I hope I can convey my anguish and repentance. I don't want to die, she says. Her gaze is fastened on the black window-panes in front of us, panning faces back. The words she says are aimed at the window. I look at her reflection and she looks at mine. Scaring her has distanced her from her mother's death, but it wasn't what I'd set out to do. Actions and consequences. She jerks her head like an ostrich, clicks her tongue against her teeth as if calling for lost pets. She says, we both are lacking some parents, Simon. What she wants me to say, I understand it now, is big brother.

Beneath the innocence, a rasp issues from her throat. I take the CD out of my pocket. My throat is thick with guilt, and something more. We both lack something else, yeh? I say.

She looks over curiously. Did he give you that, Simon?

Who do you mean? My laugh is brittle too; with a rough flick, I send it spiralling, clattering against the underside of padded seats. In the deep bass-rumble of the London Underground carriages, I remember Chinese Pygmalion as an episode, an aftertaste – that of an illicit gunpowder thrill – to which I turn because there's a new expanded certainty of who I am, and in which I lose myself.

GREEN

Roelof Bakker

I died last month. Didn't have time to say goodbye. Instead of catching a bus, a bus caught me. It hit me as I crossed the road and crushed my bones, flattened my insides.

Mine was an app-related death. I was playing *Word Jigsaw* on my phone. At Bigger Level. Occupied eyes. Looking down, not up.

I was hooked on word games and word apps. Through *Match Up* and *Word of the Day* I'd collect new words, discovered double meanings. Take 'flatulent' for example. I thought it just meant wind escaping, farting. I never realized it's a writing style too. Flatulent writing. Pompous. Pretentious.

It sounds dramatic but I died because of a love of words. Sadly, I can't remember the last word I read.

*

Strange, to be at your own funeral. Here I am at the chapel of a north London crematorium hiding inside an Eco Banana Round Woven Coffin.

Hushed voices, then speeches. I didn't realize quite how loved and liked I was. Nothing religious, thank God. Then the coffin started to move as if I was alive. I felt like shouting: resurrection, resurrection, the second coming!

But no such thing. The coffin slowly disappeared from view. Piano music echoed through the chapel. Erik Satie, *Gymnopédie No.1*, a good choice. Well done, Dad.

The coffin descended and went straight to the cremation chamber. I could feel the heat, bloody scorching. Took more than two hours for the job to be done. Afterwards there was no trace of the Eco Banana Round Woven Coffin. All gone, evaporated.

My remains were ground down like Arabica coffee beans and put into a Sunflower Banana Ashes Casket, the same weave as the coffin.

It stood on the unused dining room table at my parents' house. Next to a large bowl of fruit, wrinkly apples, rotten oranges and spotty bananas. I could never understand why my parents bought fruit.

There were bouquets in glass vases, condolence cards and framed photographs documenting different stages of my life.

A baby in a pram.
A proud seven-year-old showing off his first bicycle.
With my three sisters on Brighton Pier, our bodies distorted in the laughing mirrors (long gone).
A family holiday in France, baguettes stuffed under our arms.
Jack and I at the football club, covered in mud.
Happy days!

In the centre of the display, me and Glenda, a nurse from Cardiff. We met in hospital at the A&E. The Whittington in Archway. I'd broken my arm after being knocked off my bike. She had looked after me, made me smile. I fell in love with her pale blue eyes and bright ginger hair. We ended up going out for three years. Then she went cold on me. Turned out she'd fallen for one of the doctors, an obstetrician, busy with pregnancy and babies. Guess they have some now themselves. We didn't keep in touch. She came to my funeral. Sat alone.

Because of the recession and cut-backs, I'd lost my job as Human Resources Admin Assistant at Islington Council. I moved back in with my parents. I tried hard but I didn't succeed in finding another job, got some interviews, but nothing more. It had been three years since I'd last worked.

Dad had gone through the stuff in my room. He found the poetry I'd written after Glenda had left me. I was wondering what the point of it all was. Feeling sad, angry, hurt. Tried to write my feelings down.

So I fell in love with words, with language. My dictionary became my best friend. I'd go to the library to attend author readings and joined the North London Poetry Society.

Funnily enough, I wrote a poem about cremation, for a group project of the Society. I read it at one of our meetings.

Green,
green field –
peaceful,
still;

ready to embrace
my last will.

*Reciting words
patiently
rehearsed.*

*Ashes scattered,
solemnly
dispersed.*

   *

 *

     *

Three weeks after the funeral, scatter-day arrived. As I hadn't left instructions, it was decided to free my ashes on Hampstead Heath. I had shared many good times with my family there.

Dad had taught me to swim in the men's pond. Ice cold water. Me wearing a big rubber ring around my little chest as he guided me on. Sometimes I piggy-backed and lay on top of him, with my arm`s straddled around his neck. Soon, I'd learnt to swim on my own. Dad next to me, watching over me.

Off they went on a Friday afternoon. Dad, Mum, my sisters and the Sunflower Banana Ashes Casket. Early February, bone-chilling wind. It had been raining and the Heath was muddy, slippery.

Kitted out in Wellingtons and matching kagools, my family looked like a squadron on a mission to liberate me from the casket.

They walked up to the top of the hill by Kenwood House, a special spot, where on a bright day, you get a glorious picture-postcard view of the city.

Wellies got sucked into the soil as Dad recited my poem

beautifully, with impeccable timing. The North London Poetry Society would have been proud.

One by one they scooped a handful of ashes. Allowed the wind to carry me away.

*

*

*

*

*

*

FREE HARDCORE

Dan Powell

Bill opens the door to find two lads on his front step. One is tall and pale skinned, his face a jumble of spots and blackheads, the other squat and fat, his face greasy with sweat. Both wear faded, once-black t-shirts, the band logos crinkled and disintegrating. Both are smirking and seem, to Bill, about to laugh.

'We've come about the sign,' says tall and spotty. He jigs and looks back over each shoulder, then grins again at Bill.

'Yeah, the sign,' says the fat lad. He points back down the drive, to the edge of the road where an off-cut of MDF hangs nailed to the fence. A girlish giggle escapes him like a burp.

Bill looks the lads up and down. 'The sign?' he says.

Both boys answer. Both boys nod. Both boys grin. 'Yeah, the sign,' they say.

Bill looks them down and up. They both bounce on the balls of their feet and grin back at him.

'Fuck off,' Bill says and slams the door.

He takes the stairs two at a time and stops at the landing window to watch the pair trudge back up the drive. They stop when they reach the sign and stare back at the house. Bill thinks they can see him in the window but isn't sure until the fat lad flicks him the Vs and the spotty one kicks the sign from the fence post.

'Who were that at the door?'

Helen is stood at the bottom of the stairs, a full laundry basket clutched to her belly. From where he stands Bill can't help but see down her blouse, to where her bra cups her breast.

'No one,' he says.

Bill painted the sign himself, tongue poked between his lips in concentration. The black gloss dripped in streaks across the MDF as he slapped each letter down. Now he takes a nail from the four gripped between his teeth and, pinching it between forefinger and thumb, he hammers. Thump. Thump. Thump. Thump. He takes the three remaining nails in turn and pounds them in, then drops the hammer to the ground. He stands back for a moment, checks that the sign is level, then grips its sides and pulls. The sign does not budge.

He hefts the hammer in his fist and walks back along the drive. A cairn-like pile of stone and broken brick looms into view as he rounds the house and he compares the size of it to that of the building. He cannot tell if the mound is any bigger today than yesterday, at least not by sight, but in his gut he knows that it has grown.

Bill lies in bed and listens to the thick hiss of traffic noise from the B-road that skirts the edges of the adjacent fields. Helen is curled up on her side of the bed, her back to him. He is sure she is asleep. The curtains are open and he watches clouds drift across the waxing gibbous moon that hovers behind the house. The moonlight illuminates the contours of Helen's blanketed body and the sweeping curve of her hips exacerbates the erection that is keeping Bill awake.

He shoves his left hand down into his pyjamas and squeezes his balls and the room darkens and remains dark. He hesitates with his right hand and is about to grab his penis when the room lightens and he sees Helen is staring at him.

'What are you doing?' she hisses.

He slips his hand from inside his pyjamas and rests it upon his stomach. 'Nothing,' he says.

Helen closes her eyes and turns away from him and back onto her side. 'Go to sleep,' she says.

A middle-aged man in a brown mackintosh, his collar turned up against the elements, is stood at the front door. Rain plasters the man's mousy blond hair to his forehead in wet curls.

'I've come about the sign,' the man in the mackintosh says.

Bill looks him up and down then scans the drive. A tired, rusting Ford Fiesta is parked next to his own van. 'Where's your wagon?' he says, 'You'll need a wagon.' But the man doesn't seem to hear him over the falling rain so he raises his voice. 'You best come in,' he says.

Raindrops stream down the man's coat. They spatter and darken the carpet at his feet.

'How much is it you want?' Bill asks.

'Depends,' says the man and he leans toward Bill and leers. 'Is it the good stuff?'

'The good stuff?'

'You're a man of the world, you've been around a bit,' the man says and he winks at Bill. 'You know...the good stuff.'

'Who's that you're talking too?' Helen calls from upstairs.

Bill turns and looks up. She is leaning over the banister above him and the light from the landing window makes a silhouette of her. The outline of her breasts steals his breath.

'I said who's that you're talking to?'

'Just some bloke come about the sign,' Bill says.

'Is that the Mrs?' The man is beside Bill now and, as Helen disappears back into the upstairs, he winks again.

'What?'

'Just asking if that's your good lady wife.' The man winks once more and this time the leer of it stays in his face.

Bill looks the man down and up. 'You here about the sign or not?'

'Oh yes, yes. It's the good stuff, yes? It's good? Is it? Is it good? Is it?'

The man nudges at Bill with his elbow and Bill flinches.

'What're you talking about?'

'It's proper, yeah. The proper stuff.'

The man's grin jabs a flash of sickness into Bill's gut and he grabs the collar of his mackintosh and drags him down the hall.

'Get out,' Bill shouts and shoves the man down the front step, sends him sprawling face first into a puddle. Bill waits until the man in the mackintosh has picked himself up and climbed back into his car, then he slams the front door.

'Everything okay down there?'

Bill hears Helen calling but he does not reply.

Bill folds his work trousers and shirt and places them on the old armchair squatting in the corner of the bedroom. He climbs into bed, lies still and listens to the water running and floorboards creaking in the bathroom. He waits.

Once Helen is in bed beside him he sidles across the mattress, slips his arm around her and rests his palm on the soft flab of her tummy. He holds it there, feels her tense at his touch, but he does not dare speak. When she says nothing he pulls his hand back, rolls onto his side.

'I'm tired,' Helen says. He does not reply. He tries but cannot think of anything to say and anyway, Helen is once more already asleep.

He gives up trying to sleep. He slips downstairs and grabs his mobile phone and wallet from where they sit on the telephone table by the back door. Once in the living room he closes the door behind him. Sat in the dark he cocks his head and listens to the house. Only once he is sure all is silent does he dial.

You are just seconds away from hot chat with some dirty, dirty girls, the phone breathes into his ear. The voice is husky, and lusty, but this does not hide the deadness of the recording. *Press 1 to hear the list of all the available girls*, it says. *Press 2 to be connected to the first available girl. Or, if you already know who you want to be connected to, enter the number of your favourite girl on your keypad now.*

Bill pulls the phone from his ear and taps the number 2. There is a buzz on the line for a moment or two and he pulls the phone from his ear and listens for sounds in the house. The ringing from the earpiece of his phone is low and distant and then stops.

He puts the phone back to his ear. *Hello lover*, a voice says, *This is Tina. Are you feeling horny tonight?*

'Yes,' Bill says, 'Yes I am.'

Bill wakes before it is light, unlocks the back door and steps outside. The garden and the fields beyond the post and rail fencing are lit up by the full moon. Dark silhouettes of trees and hedges mark the boundary lines of the surrounding land. He glances back up at the house, his eyes drawn to the bedroom window, then steps across the yard to the heap of broken brick and stone. It has grown since yesterday, he is sure of it. Its height more than matches the house now and he is sure its circumference has spread. He crosses to where his mini-digger squats hunched up, the bucket turned into the crook of the articulated arm, and he hauls himself into the cab. He places his hands on the controls and stares out at the mass of broken brick.

Bill spends the day loading his trailer and hauling it to the tip. He pays the dumping costs without complaint. Each time he drives the unladen tractor and trailer back along the single-track roads he feels lighter in himself. After dumping the third load he pulls onto the drive to find an elderly man in builder's overalls waiting for him.

'I've come about your sign,' the old man says.

Bill sighs and jumps down from his tractor. A drop-sided wagon is parked next to the mini-digger. He does not look at the mound. He refuses to check if it has grown again.

'How much d'yer want?' he says.

'Fill it up,' the old man says.

Helen brings out tea just as Bill finishes leveling the load with the bottom of the digger's bucket. He climbs down from the cab and she smiles at him as she hands him his mug. She brushes his cheek with her hand and he feels himself at once loosen and bristle at her touch. He knows he should say something but cannot frame his feelings into words.

Helen returns to the house and the two men sit on the tracks of the mini-digger. They sip at their tea and stare at the mound of stone and broken brick that still remains behind Bill's house. Above them the sky begins to cloud and darken.

'Don't look like we've made a dent in it,' the old man says and laughs.

'It never does,' Bill says.

The bedroom is dark; the night sky outside is encased in cloud. Bill can hear Helen breathing. He can feel, through the mattress, the rhythmic rise and fall of her chest. He lies still and listens and is almost asleep himself when he thinks he hears the other sound. He climbs from the bed and steps to the window and holds himself still. He can feel the mound of broken stone and brick brooding outside and he listens for the sound of weight massing in the dark.

THE MORNING PERSON

Adrian Cross

The morning person was up at seven bright as a button, for the last time, though it wasn't until mid-afternoon that I finally did away with him. After all there's efficacy in taking advantage of someone's worst time constitutionally. He was not alone in feeling listless and drowsy at that time, add to this the summer heat, and you can begin to see my reasoning.

It should never have got to this point if I'm honest about it. After all he had given up rapping at my door, intoning 'Rise and shine!' with, what I call, an unfettered Hitler Youth spirit. It was unjust when you think about it, but the damage had been done. Each day as I eventually lurched out of the bedroom rubbing my eyes, as if a bomb had been detonated, I always found him breezily spreading his toast with honey. And as the dust settled on me one morning, I was able to plot his downfall in hard-won monochrome clarity. You could say I'd woken up and smelt the coffee.

I'm a homeopath. I can make a remedy out of almost nothing. A consultation ranges far and wide like a little gecko over the ceiling. The patient sits opposite, often with his palms together between closed thighs as if in prayer, and, I, the tiny lizard tease out a personal history and a template of emotional wellbeing. It's a scarcely known fact that if you knew what went into the elixirs of your conventional medicine cupboard you might never open it again, just as reality is removed in an aeroplane by the craven smiles of the stewardess and the laboratory presentation of the food. The whole planet simply consists of chemicals re-organising themselves. You're not that distinct from a bus shelter in essence. I have ground the casing of a mobile phone to cure a client of the constant voices he was hearing. You'll see that it works. Once I treated a stiff neck. Within hours the patient felt a tingling and the discomfort vanished through the top of his head like a succubus spirited out.

I am heavily prone to insomnia. And I knew next door he slept contentedly. You can sense it can't you? Beauty sleep as a landscape. A warm inviting mist that hangs over the sluggard's bed. So while he was sound next door I was almost weeping with distress in my curdled sheets. I would shuffle out to his door, tap softly, suggest a game of snooker and he'd rise gently out of his slumber like a hologram, politely decline and slip blissfully back to sleep.

One night however I lay rigid, the hairs on the back of my neck stood on end, and this is how the germ of a solution came. The night sky cast its luminescent sin into the room. In a lucid dream, on the spit of my consciousness, I saw a limousine draw up outside, jet black naturally. A gloved hand opened the door and waited for me. I got out of bed, wrapped a coat around myself, floated out of the window and into the car. Opposite was seated an old man, centuries old, putting down tarot cards. The chauffeur drove us to the club. We secured a table for ourselves, the only sound the scratching of the chalk on the end of my cue and the clack of a shot from another table. The light filtered the dust above the baize and it seemed to me that the cream glove of the chauffeur was placing the balls with the eerie precision of the match referee, each one given a light fingertip caress. With infinite patience he arranged the colours like the planets, as if they orbited around me. Then the blue rolled forward of its own accord and I awoke from my reverie. As I did so I realized that in my sleep I had concocted a plan. I suppose you'd say I'm N-stage syphilitic, the state of mind in homeopathic parlance that declares 'it's either me or him'.

I'd offer him a session for free. Unfortunately my lodger was always in exemplary health. However, crucially, I had divined a certain morbidity in him. He once told me he had the urge to throw himself under a passing train while idling on the platform, a desire he was at a loss to explain. Then of course, I would create a remedy for perfection. Perfection as that infernal sickness: a vain, futile striving of the human heart. Coming up with a remedy is a matter of matching something to the client's frequency at that particular time and it must either be the same pitch or the polar opposite, nothing in between. I would administer a substance which would generate the symptoms of perfection in a healthy person, but trigger the very opposite in his state of mind. All I needed to do was find out where that perfection already lay in the world as we know it. Of course there was enormous risk involved. I would literally be piloting a remedy on him. Then again, if it failed, I could simply pass it off as the wrong cure.

You see homeopathic remedies are infinitesimally diluted to render them free from side effects, so they are the perfect murder tool! Virtually undetectable! The beauty of it is staggering. I had hoped not to leave any trace whatsoever, but I soon realized I could only obtain the substances I needed through a slither of malpractice. I almost booked a plane to Florence, fancied myself in one of those heist movies slipping into the Uffizi unnoticed, eluding all their systems to chisel off a chunk of Michelangelo's David: perhaps the tender, button mushroom penis. I soon chuckled to myself at how fanciful I was being. I really mustn't get carried away. I had never taken anyone's life before and this was no time for getting big for my boots. No, the best I could do was rummage in the marketplace of botox, collagen and silicon. I could have just given him an overdose, but I wanted to be more fiendish, more subtle. I asked my surgeon chum Paul Devros if I could have some of the tissue from a breast reduction. He let me have it within a week.

I got up fresh as a daisy on my appointed morning. The sunlight was streaming in, tarnished only by the heap of dishes in the sink. I could hear him splashing about in the shower. When he came out we exchanged cursory 'good mornings'. Not because there was any coldness on his part, just that he was eager to proceed with his regimes. These consisted of some grunting workouts followed by a little yoga and meditation. He was working at home that day and, before he went to the living room to boot up his laptop, he turned and said, 'Shall we have that consultation later?'

At that moment the words stuck in my throat and I almost cancelled the whole thing. But I swallowed hard, feeling a dryness in my throat and replied somewhat timidly, 'I think we should.'

I tell you I didn't know where to put myself for the rest of that morning. I devoted some attention to the cat, but, as you know, they soon tire of you. The tapping of his fingers on the keyboard became a kind of torture. I tried to read, but of course I couldn't. When I look back it wasn't so much that I disliked him. In fact he was, on reflection, a very reasonable human being, and, until that day, I never felt any actual hatred for him. But once you have decided to terminate your relationship with someone it becomes a sine qua non to loathe your victim, in order that you can go through with the act, just like the ending of a marriage.

The point is I felt superior to the morning person, though now it occurs to me that, possibly at root, I felt myself inferior. The mind is such a complex scramble of myth and bunkum one never really knows does one?

I picked at the previous day's stew and realized the only thing to ease the tension was a wholesome swim, so I went into the living room and boldly informed him that I was putting our session back one hour. When I returned he was waiting for me in the garden. He put down his magazine and said, 'I thought we could enjoy the sun.'

'An excellent idea,' I beamed.

We both let the rays warm our faces and were silent for a time. I looked at the flowers crawling up and sprawling over the fence. Bees hovered round them and swifts darted across the sky. It was as idyllic as could be in all honesty.

He began by telling me how ashamed he was of his body, and how this brought out a tickly cough. It was the first time I had seen his serenity and self-assurance cloud in the nine months that he'd lodged with me. He told me how his 'weediness' preoccupied him. He invited me to imagine a day, much like today, and that I was strolling on the common with a wife and child when they were threatened by a stranger intent on doing them harm.

'Would I be prepared to physically defend them?' he asked me.

I replied that it didn't really matter, because I could use my guile to disarm the assailant. He laughed and said I was being unrealistic. It was a bitter laugh directed at himself. It was clear I had to be careful not to make him feel so much better that he declined the remedy I had for him. I needn't have worried. He really was quite in the dumps. A light breeze rustled the plants and I reached into my box of remedies and pulled out the similia similibus curentur. I was staggered by how calm I felt. The vial looks so innocuous filled with tiny white pills. I handed the one at the top to him and asked him to place it under his tongue.

And then it was done.

I told him it would make him feel just perfect, but of course it was crafted from a diminution, not an augmentation.

Then I made my excuses, saying it was chilly now the sun had dipped behind the clouds, and went in. It was only when I was shut in my room that I drew in a deep breath. I felt that I needed to be out again and packed my swimming things once more. Instead, though, I went to the kitchen. I glanced at him, still out there reading, and took a bottle of whisky and a glass back to my room. I lay on the futon and drank steadily. Before I passed out I heard him shuffle past the door.

When I came round it was dark, about eight I think. With a throbbing head I gathered up the swimming gear again and headed out the door. From the car I could see him in the first floor window at the computer with his head in his hands, its screen dormant. When I returned he was in his room and all was quiet. I played some Handel and drifted off to sleep. In the morning I found him dead, a jar of painkillers by the bed. Of course we say in homeopathy that after so many dilutions what remains in the water of the original substance is a kind of memory. Oh yes, we believe very strongly in memory. So savagely he took his own life, and I still have the vial, but I can live with its inconsequential trace.

ONE HOUR,
THREE TIMES A WEEK

Sonal Kohli

The house had two gates. There was a large rust coloured one, past which Mr. Lamba could see nothing. It seemed like the entrance to the factory. A few metres ahead was a small white gate with square holes at the top. Mr. Lamba walked his scooter to the smaller gate and parked it. He peeked in through the square grille. There was an oval, grassless lawn and an empty veranda. He tried the doorbell, but the switch was stuck. Mr. Lamba lifted the latch and went inside.

He knocked at the glass door. In the kitchen, to his left, a yellow fridge hummed loudly. There were two Coca-Cola bottle magnets on the fridge.

A boy of eight or nine came to the door.

'Is your father at home?' Mr. Lamba asked.

'He's at the factory. You should use the other gate.' The boy was barefoot.

'Is your mother at home?'

'Yes. Wait.' He ran inside, leaving Mr. Lamba standing there holding his helmet.

The grassless lawn was lined with rose shrubs on one side.

Two children's cycles leant against the veranda wall.

'Yes?' The mother appeared at the door. She had a round face, just like her son. She wore a blue sari with big, pink flowers on it.

'I'm Suresh Lamba.' He cleared his throat. 'I'm a school teacher, and I provide private tuitions as well. Your husband, I think, left his card for me at Satnam Stationers.'

'Ah, yes. He spoke about it. Come in, please.'

The living area was long and narrow, like a passage, with a dining table on the near side and black sofas on the far one. He and the mother settled down on the sofas. There was a money plant in the corner with large, waxy leaves.

'My sister-in-law and I are looking for a tutor for our sons,' the mother said. 'They are the same age.'

'Would you like me to tutor them together or separately?'

'You can teach them together and charge for one-and-a-half pupils. That's how their last tutor worked.'

'Which class are they in?'

'They've just started third grade.' Then she asked, 'How long have you been teaching, sir?'

'It's been twenty-five years. My subjects are Math and English, but I can help with others as well.'

'Okay. But they are a bit naughty, so you'll have to be strict.'

'Don't worry about that.' Mr. Lamba laughed and adjusted his glasses.

She called out to the boys.

Three doors on the opposite wall led into the bedrooms. Mr. Lamba folded his arms over his stomach and waited for the boys to emerge. On the showcase a glass heron bent and rose periodically as it sipped from a trough. It was a lulling movement.

An old woman came out of the middle room and sat down on the sofa.

'Namaste,' Mr. Lamba said.

The woman nodded but said nothing. There was a slit in the side of her nose where she must have once worn a heavy nose ring.

'Anuj and Raghu's new tutor,' the young woman said to the older one.

The boys came and stood by the mother. 'This is Raghu,' she said, pointing to the boy with full cheeks. He was still barefoot. 'And this is my sister-in-law's son, Anuj.' Anuj had a thin, dusky face and a staple-sized scar on his chin. The cousins smiled at Mr. Lamba. Both were missing some teeth.

'So we start next Monday, boys?' Mr. Lamba said.

The boys nodded.

*

Mr. Lamba got out of bed and stretched his arms. There was grey-black hair in his armpits. At home it was his habit to wear just vest and pyjamas, and when winter came he wrapped a shawl over the vest. He arched his back, straightened, and twisted to the right then left. His son was still sleeping on the other divan. Mr. Lamb folded the top sheet and patted the pillow.

He made two cups of tea and took one to his mother. He helped her sit up.

'Everything okay, Roop Kumar?' She addressed Mr. Lamba as her long dead brother, the only person she seemed to remember.

'Yes, everything okay.'

He took his cup outside and sat in a chair and drank the tea. He contemplated the two sparrows that pecked at each other on the boundary wall. It was warm for April. The sun shone brightly. For the last week, he had been reminding himself to water the basil that sat next to the gate. The leaves were turning brown at the edges.

The newspaper boy threw the paper, rolled and secured with a rubber band, over the gate. It landed with a thud.

Mr. Lamba read the headlines as he finished the tea. Sikh militants had again attacked a bus of Hindu pilgrims in Punjab. They shot the conductor and two male passengers. Mr. Lamba skimmed through the details.

He put the cups in the sink and took his mother to the bathroom. Her skin had become loose and hung from her bones in thin pleats. A maid came twice a week to give her a bath.

He dusted the dining table and chairs, the switch board, and the centre table between the two divans. With light strokes he brushed the crotchet wall hanging his wife had made one winter. He wiped the cupboards in his mother's room and the cramped side tables. There were only two bedrooms in the house. After his wife passed away two years ago, he gave his room to his daughter. He could hear her working in the kitchen. He cleaned the window panes before joining her.

He kneaded the dough and rolled the chapattis, while she prepared vegetables. His son was in the bathroom, splashing himself with mugs full of water. He was an accountant in a small firm. Mr. Lamba shared his shirts with him. They were snug for Mr. Lamba but loose for his son, who at twenty-three was still lanky. The only household errand the son did was to put buttons on the shirts whenever they went missing.

Mr. Lamba packed his lunch, got ready, and left for work.

*

Mr. Lamba arrived at five sharp for the first tutorial. He parked his scooter outside the smaller gate. The road was dusty and busy with traffic, and factory workers walked home carrying tin lunchboxes. Across the road was Voltas' Delhi plant. The facade was painted orange and cream.

Mr. Lamba tried the doorbell, then lifted the latch and went inside.

In the kitchen, the cook was chopping vegetables. He wore grey overalls, like a factory worker.

Mr. Lamba knocked briefly at the glass door and stepped inside. He found Anuj and Raghu jumping from one sofa to the next, like a pair of kangaroos. He cleared his throat.

'Good evening, sir.' The boys climbed down.

'Good evening.' Mr. Lamba sat on the long sofa. 'Bring your books. And you put on your slippers,' he added to Raghu. The boy had left dusty paw marks on the black seats.

He placed his helmet and the cloth bag, in which he carried his lunch and school notebooks, under the coffee table. He could hear faint notes of a ghazal coming from the room near the sofas.

The boys brought their school bags and settled on either side of Mr. Lamba. Raghu was wearing his mother's flip-flops, which were two sizes big for him.

'We'll start with English.' He asked them to read a page each from the text.

Both the boys read haltingly and Anuj had trouble stringing the letters together. Mr. Lamba realised he would have to work hard with them. He explained the text and dictated answers to the questions at the back, while the boys took notes kneeling by the coffee table. The ghazal continued to play lightly.

The cook brought a cup of tea.

'Can you please bring some biscuits?' Mr. Lamba said to him. 'I get acidity, if I don't eat with my evening tea.'

'I'll get some for you, sir,' Anuj said jumping up.

'You study.' He pressed Anuj down by the shoulder and smiled at the cook.

The music stopped and a woman emerged from the room. 'They are always trying to run away from their books,' she said. 'Namaste, sir. I'm Anuj's mother.' She looked at the books spread on the table. 'His grammar and spellings need special attention.'

'Don't worry.' Mr. Lamba picked the skin off the tea. 'He has good hand writing though.'

Anuj stuck out his tongue at his mother.

'That's true.' She smiled and returned to her room. This time she shut the door

Mr. Lamba dunked the biscuits and sipped the tea. The boys memorised the answers they had noted down, sitting with their feet up on the sofa. On the right hand wall was a set of double doors with a brass bolt across the middle. 'Is this a cupboard?' Mr. Lamba asked. He had missed it on the first visit.

The cousins laughed. Raghu slid off the sofa and unbolted the doors.

Mr. Lamba shifted his weight to see. A set of stairs led up and then disappeared into darkness. An old toaster sat on the first step. On the other side were pairs of worn shoes. A badminton racket lay on the step above, and above that a torn cushion, with the sponge showing.

'The stairs go up to the terrace,' Raghu said.

'The terrace door is burnt like Mrs. Venkatraman's arm, sir,' Anuj said.

'Who is Mrs. Venkatraman?'

'She teaches Math at school,' Raghu said.

Mr. Lamba imagined the shrivelled skin of Mrs. Venkatraman's burnt arm.

'Our old cook was smoking a beedi and he threw it and the newspapers at the top of the stairs caught fire,' Anuj told Mr. Lamba.

'We sometimes take our bicycles to the terrace, sir,' Raghu said. 'The terrace is small, but if we go round in circles, we can cycle for a long time without stopping.'

'Is there no park close by where you can go?'

Raghu shook his head. He shut the door and came and sat in his place. 'We are not allowed to go out of the house alone, sir, not even to look for our cricket balls.'

Mr. Lamba nodded. It was an industrial area. There were factories up and down the road and no houses in the vicinity. Workers lingered at tea stalls and Mr. Lamba had seen some smoking outside factory gates. It wouldn't be safe for the boys to be out by themselves, but he could understand how suffocating it must be for them to be cooped at home. He looked from Anuj to Raghu. They were trying to memorise the answers, eyes clenched, rocking back and forth. He wished he could take them out one afternoon but felt that it would be inappropriate.

The grandmother came and sat at the dining table. Mr. Lamba put aside the cup and resumed the lesson.

*

A week later, on his way back from the tuition, Mr. Lamba stopped at Satnam Stationers. With the helmet under his arm, he waited while Satnam Singh packed red and green glaze paper, gum and golden sprinkle for a girl who stood on this side of the counter. Satnam slipped a pink flier into the bag before handing it to the girl.

'How are you?' Mr. Lamba said, as the girl skipped away.

'Same as ever.' Satnam lifted the counter flap and Mr. Lamba walked in. He sat down on the extra stool. Behind him, next to a jar of pencils, hung the pink flier he had put there a month ago asking parents and students to contact him for home tuitions. Below the note was the sketch of a man on a scooter. Mr. Lamba looked bulky even in the sketch.

'I got the tuition job,' he said.

'Very good, very good, sir.' Satnam patted Mr. Lamba's back. He had a ball pen tucked between his ear and black turban. 'We need to celebrate.' He sent the shop help to get tea and samosas.

'I'm tutoring two little boys. Thank you, Satnam.' He took the stationer's hand and clapped it with his palm. It was Satnam's idea that Mr. Lamba start home tuitions. After his wife's death, he found it difficult to pass the time at home. He would correct the school notebooks, put a chair outside and watch the street, come and lie on the divan, but the long evenings refused to come to an end. Satnam even allowed him to put his phone number on the flier, as Mr. Lamba did not have a phone at home.

They ate the samosas. A hot breeze was blowing, making the trees rustle. The two talked about the weather and the long power cuts and about Rakesh Sharma's satellite call to Mrs. Gandhi from outer space. Like always, they kept away from the subject of politics, the militancy in Punjab and the Sikhs' demand for a separate nation. Satnam brushed the samosa crumbs off the counter.

Mr. Lamba finished the tea, bought a packet of red ball pens and left for home.

*

Raghu and Anuj lay on the sofa, watching cricket. Their grandmother and Anuj's mother were at the dining table, playing cards, possibly Rummy. The mother had a white bandage around her palm. Mr. Lamba wanted to ask what happened, but he only cleared his throat.

'Namaste, sir,' she said. The grandmother glanced at the clock. The boys sprang from the sofa, turned off the television, and scrambled to the room for their books.

Mr. Lamba said Namaste to the mother and grandmother and went to sit at the long sofa.

The boys settled on either side of him. 'Good evening, sir,' they said.

'Take out your Math books. We'll do unitary method sums today.'

He told Raghu to read out the first problem.

'If ten chocolates cost twenty rupees, how much would three chocolates cost?'

'So Anuj.' Mr. Lamba put his arm around the boy. 'What do you think? Would it cost less than twenty or more?'

Anuj stroked his chin. 'Less?'

'Yes. Good. Now to solve this problem, we need to first find the price of one chocolate.' He wrote down:

10 chocolates cost Rs. 20

∴ 1 chocolate costs 20 ÷ 10

'In unitary method, we first find the price of one unit,' he repeated. 'Now to calculate the price of three chocolates, we multiply the above by three. And there's your answer: six rupees.'

The boys nodded.

Anuj read out the next problem and Mr. Lamba's pen worked fluently on the page dividing and multiplying. They went through five sums together.

'Did you get that?' He looked at the boys over his glasses. He wrote them questions to practise. The boys did the calculations kneeling by the coffee table. Mr. Lamba sharpened four pencils and set them on the table in a neat row. He folded his arms over his stomach then and waited for tea. The glass heron bent and rose.

'I'll be back. Continue with your calculations.' He went to the toilet.

When he returned, Raghu was wearing his helmet and riding the arm of the sofa, with Anuj trying to snatch the helmet off his head.

'What's this?' Mr. Lamba said.

Raghu took off the helmet and the boys slipped back into their seats.

Mr. Lamba sat down between them and put the helmet under the coffee table. The helmet was scratched, and its white under shell showed here and there. He cuffed the back of the boys' heads.

'Our last tutor, Mr. Bhaskar, used to wear a thick bracelet, sir,' Raghu said, without looking up from his notebook. 'Every time he slapped us, his bracelet hit our jaw hard. It hurt more than the slap, sir.'

'Okay, do your sums.' His stomach growled. The cousins snickered. Mr. Lamba wondered if the cook would bring tea today, but based on the past month, he knew that neither the cook nor the tea could be counted on.

'You know, sir, a monkey bit my mother's hand,' Anuj said.

'How did that happen?' Mr. Lamba pushed back his glasses.

'She had just washed her face at the sink in the veranda,' he said, getting cross-legged on the floor, 'and she raised her hand to get the towel from the rail, when this fat monkey sitting on the wall bit her.'

Mr. Lamba tsked tsked.

'She had to get injections,' Raghu said and laughed. Anuj laughed too.

'Okay, enough. Now let me see your notebooks.'

'Two more minutes, sir,' they cried, and started to scribble furiously.

As Mr. Lamba was leaving that evening, the grandmother came out of her room. 'There are still five minutes left,' she said.

Mr. Lamba glanced at the clock. Its golden hands were shaped like arrows. 'Ah, yes.' But he wasn't sure if he should go back and tell the boys to reopen their books. 'I'll make up for it next time,' he said, and left clutching the helmet under his arm and craving his evening tea.

*

Mr. Lamba sat outside his house in vest and pyjamas. The newspaper rested on his knee. The sky was the colour of mud, and it looked like there would be a dust storm. Monsoon didn't seem far off. Children were playing hopscotch. They had drawn the grid with chalk, which they must have stolen from school. Their shorts and frocks flapped in the breeze.

His daughter returned from the stenography class. She looked at Mr. Lamba and their eyes met. She was having an affair with a man from the neighbourhood. Mr. Lamba sometimes saw him drop her back. He had short, greasy hair and looked like a wrestler with his thick shoulders and the way he held the handlebars of the bike. Mr. Lamba didn't have enough money to get the dowry together, so he stayed quiet and let the affair continue. She was wearing maroon lipstick and hoop earrings. Mr. Lamba turned his attention to the sports page.

Dust and grit started to blow down the lane. The children laughed and shrieked and ran indoors. Mr. Lamba too picked up his chair and went in.

In the kitchen, he and his daughter stood side by side, while she cooked vegetables and he made chapattis, without exchanging a word.

*

Mr. Lamba arrived for the lesson at three that afternoon. It was Raghu's birthday and his friends were coming over in the evening to celebrate. When he passed the kitchen, he saw the mothers and the cook busy with preparations and the slabs crowded with dishes and pans.

The living room walls were decorated with strips of crepe paper. A bunch of balloons hung from the fan over the dining table. 'Happy Birthday,' he wished Raghu. He removed from the cloth bag a box of crayons and an abridged and illustrated copy of *The Adventures of Tom Sawyer*. 'For you.'

'Thank you, sir!'

The cousins sat side by side and flipped through the illustrations.

Mr. Lamba made them do maps that day, to keep it light because of the boy's birthday. 'On the top, write "India and its Neighbours" in block letters.'

'Do you remember my birthday, sir?' Anuj asked, as he lettered in Bhutan.

'It's not for another two months. Do your work.' He had already decided to bring him *Robinson Crusoe*. Satnam had a copy in the shop. Mr. Lamba didn't read much himself, not beyond the texts he taught at school, but *The Last Leaf* was his favourite story. Every year when he read it out to the eighth grade, his heart trembled like the painted leaf on the tree.

The cook brought tea, and a cutlet and jalebi in a quarter plate.

Mr. Lamba sipped at the tea and directed the boys to mark Arabian Sea, Bay of Bengal and Indian Ocean. Then while the boys coloured the waters blue, he sat back and bit into the treats. The jalebi was thick and syrupy. He licked his fingers when he was done.

The hour came to an end and he got up to leave.

'Sir,' Raghu said, as he folded the map and put it away in a notebook. 'Come to the terrace. I want to show you how high we've got our kite. We've tied it to the water tank.'

Mr. Lamba laughed. 'Okay. Go wear your slippers first.'

Anuj slid the bolt and Mr. Lamba followed the boys up the stairs. More than the kite, he wanted to see the burnt door. The stairwell smelled dusty. There was no light bulb, and books and newspapers lay in corners, making the stairs narrower. Mr. Lamba side stepped a flat football. Finally the boys pushed open the door at the top and ran on to the terrace. The door was black, sooty. Mr. Lamba ran his palm over its uneven surface. The wood had cracked and peeled in many places. Splinters pricked his skin. He felt sorry for the door and for Mrs. Venkatraman. He briefly inhaled its burnt odour before following his students to the terrace.

The kite was nowhere on the sky. A coil of thread lay near the water tank. Raghu and Anuj were wrestling each other. Mr. Lamba went to stand by the parapet. Beyond the factories were clumps of green groves.

*

Every evening before dinner, Mr. Lamba took two pegs of whiskey, a cheap brew that he bought from the government run store. It was his habit to eat a cucumber as he drank. When his wife was alive she would slice the cucumber for him. Now he cut it thickly, without taking off the skin. He sat on the divan drinking and eating the salad. It was raining. Drops slipped down the window panes. Mr. Lamba watched the lizards play on the wall.

*

The toilet was to one side of the house, in a narrow alley that connected the veranda to the factory. The boys' fathers used the passage to come and go. Mr. Lamba could see the watchman sitting by the rust coloured gate and workers unloading sheets of steel from a truck. The boys' fathers made stainless steel utensils. The family had a steel tea set with a golden knob on the pot and a small decanter for milk. Mr. Lamba had seen the cook carry tea in it for guests.

He used the toilet, washed his hands and went back into the house.

'Five multiplied by six is thirty, not thirty-five,' he said, glancing at Raghu's notebook. He wiped his hands with his maroon handkerchief.

'Sir,' the grandmother said from the dining table where she sat doing embroidery, 'if you need to use the toilet, please go outside.'

Mr. Lamba looked up.

'Sometimes you don't flush,' she said.

Mr. Lamba felt himself going red. The boys continued with their sums, but he could feel their attention on him.

Last week she had said, 'Sir, don't sit on the same sofa every time. The centre seat has started to sag.'

Mr. Lamba now sat on a different sofa every week.

She picked up the thread box and embroidery and went to her room.

'Sir.' Raghu pointed to the middle room, then touched his temple and rotated his finger, like a screw.

Anuj laughed.

'Don't talk like that about your grandmother,' Mr. Lamba folded the handkerchief into four and put it on his knee to dry. The house was so quiet that he could hear machines whirring and the distant clatter of utensils. He folded the handkerchief further and tucked it into his pocket.

*

Mr. Lamba was in the staffroom checking notebooks when Mr. Chatterjee came in and said, 'Indira Gandhi has been shot by two of her Sikh guards.' Everyone looked at him. Chatterjee liked attention. 'She's critical. They fired at close range.' The three other teachers gathered around him to learn more. Mr. Lamba went and stood at the back of the circle.

After the lunch break, he went to the reception and gave the receptionist Raghu's father's number. The receptionist, Miss Patsy, had three fingers missing from her right hand. She dialled with the left one and passed him the receiver. Mr. Lamba cleared his throat. He told Raghu's father he would not be coming in that evening. He did not mention the attack.

*

Mr. Lamba sat at home following the live broadcast of the state funeral. It was a warm, slow day in November. The radio was on the centre table, with the antennae at forty-five degrees. The announcer said Mrs. Gandhi looked peaceful on her last journey. Mr. Lamba imagined her hooked nose sticking out of the garlands that had been put around her neck. His son lay on the opposite divan, catching up on the broadcast in between naps. The ceiling fan spun sluggishly.

Over the next few days Hindu mobs attacked Sikh neighbourhoods. Eventually a curfew was called. There was no milk at home. Mr. Lamba drank black tea for the first time. He didn't like it. He wondered if his mother could tell the difference. During the day he killed flies with the blue swatter and hoped that Satnam and his family were safe.

*

When Mr. Lamba went to Raghu and Anuj's for the tuition next week, he found the nearby Manjeet Singh factory gutted. The window panes were broken, frames hung from hinges, and shards of glass littered the compound. A portion of the building was covered in soot. A dog lay near the gate, panting.

'I hope everything was okay here,' he said to Raghu's mother. 'The mob got the Sikh factory.'

Raghu raised his head from his notebook. 'Sir, our veranda was full of burnt paper. It kept falling from the sky. I caught some bits as they fell.'

'Your name will live, Indira,' Anuj sang, 'as long as the sun and moon live.'

Mr. Lamba had heard the slogan on the radio. He cuffed the back of Anuj's head. 'Do your sums.'

'We were fine, sir,' the mother said. 'But one of our Sikh workers from the factory came today with his beard shaven and hair cut, my husband told us. He managed it just in time to escape the mob.'

Mr. Lamba imagined Satnam without his turban and beard. After the tuition, he went to the shop. The shutter was down.

For a few days Mr. Lamba heard the boys hum the slogan as they studied.

*

Mr. Lamba was driving back from the tuition. There was a greasy patch in the middle of the road. It shone and twinkled and looked like the large, elongated shadow of a kettle. He thought if he touched it, the grease would come on to his fingers and he could smell and decipher what it was. In staring at it, he forgot to avoid the patch.

He lost control of the scooter and it swerved and fell on its side. The weight came crashing down on his left leg.

A few men standing at the bus stop rushed to help. He winced when they tried to make him stand. The trouser had torn at the shin and there were some blood marks. The men stopped a passing car, put him in the back and asked the driver to take him to a clinic.

The doctor tapped Mr. Lamba's shin and knee with his knuckles and tried to rotate the ankle. He took x-rays and put the leg in a cast. He applied some ointment where Mr. Lamba had grazed his palm.

Mr. Lamba was confined to bed, like his mother. His leg looked like a cement column. The midterm exams were close and he worried about the two boys. He requested his son to call Raghu's father and tell him about the accident. He also wanted him to check on Satnam but thought that might be too much to ask.

Lying on the divan, staring at the fan go round, he wondered about the patch of grease. Was it the kerosene that the mob had used to burn the Sikhs and their properties?

*

The doorbell rang. Mr. Lamba wrapped the shawl around him, stood up with the help of the crutch and went to see who it was.

The postman gave him a brown parcel, not more than twenty grams in weight, and made him sign on a paper.

Mr. Lamba came back to the divan and opened the parcel. There was a ruled sheet inside, folded into four, a Coca-Cola bottle magnet and a pocket size cricket bat that Mr. Lamba knew was Raghu's favourite possession. He ran his fingers over the smooth wood of the bat. Its bottom corners were neatly rounded.

He put on his glasses and unfolded the letter. It was in Anuj's handwriting.

Get well soon sir. We hope the leg is not hurting too much.
We have a new tutor. He has a pointed thumb nail.
Sometimes he pinches our ears. We miss you always.
Yours obediently
Anuj and Raghu

Mr. Lamba put the letter on the table along with the bat. He limped to the kitchen with his crutch and stuck the magnet on the fridge.

INFINITY

from *a book with no name*, a work in progress

Ken Edwards

There's a room and then there's a little room and another little room off that. And then a room and a room and more rooms and then a room. And beyond that is a little room and then a large room and a room. And in through there there's another and beyond another and a room beyond. And from here they go into another room and that's the little room right there. And then the main room. The room where it happens and the room where they prepare for it to happen and the room where they go after. Then there's a room off that and a room off that and off that and off that and off that. That's where it all goes on where they go that's the room or if not the room beyond that that's where it all happens and after it happens there's another room where they go. And they all gather in that room and they talk and remark upon the room whether it's a good room or not and they remember another room was that as good a room as the room that is the room they're in or wasn't it perhaps it wasn't or perhaps it was another room they were thinking of. Perhaps they mistook that room for that room. That's the room they go into and that's the room they don't. The room they don't is still there it's locked you can't go in there unless you get a key but to do that you have to visit another room and another room and then beyond is the room where you get the key but then you have to find your way back through the first room and the second room and the third room and the fourth room so it may not be worth it. It may not be worth entering the room because there are other rooms that are just as good just as worth entering where you can do what you need to do where you can spend as much time as you like. And when you've finished you can go into the next room that's what they do go into the next room and gather there before going into the room beyond. And the room you go into before the room in which whatever happens happens is called the green room and the room you go into after is called the white room so you can easily identify it and not confuse it with the red room the blue room the yellow room the black room or the room of many colours. But the room of many colours leads into the black room and that leads to the yellow room which leads to the blue room which leads to the red room which leads to the white room and then you're back in the green room. That's where everybody goes. They go into that room and they stay there for a while and if you ask for the toilet they tell you it's beyond the next room just go left and left again and that room is the toilet and you can go to the toilet. That little room is the toilet. You can go there. Everybody goes there. And off the toilet is another toilet and then another toilet and so there are plenty of toilets in fact an infinite number of toilets so they estimate everybody can go to the toilet and everybody does. And everybody goes. Everybody is going. And when you've finished don't forget to wash your hands and then you can join everybody in the next room which is the room everybody goes to. You go right and right again to reach that room. You can't miss it. It's quite a large room. And inside that room is another room and within that an inner room which nobody really knows about but is a room that has been rumoured. The rumours spread all around the room and spill over into the adjoining rooms and then the rooms beyond that where everybody has gathered. That's where the rumours go and they go on forever. That room is locked. Is it the same room or a completely different one? Nobody can say. Nobody knows what's happening in that room but they wait in the rooms where they are or where they are urged to gather and pass the time talking and waiting until further notice for further information.

ON THE TRUTH AND LIES OF THE LOVE STORY

Charlie Hill

Hello.

How's it going?

Good, actually. Yeah. Yeah, actually, very good.

I'm ringing because I've got some news.

You'll never guess. I've met a woman. I know! I know! Seriously. It's the real thing.

How?

Oh, mate, you're not going to believe it…

Hello.

Yeah, not bad.

Actually, that's not strictly true. I've been better.

Yeah. It's one of those, I'm afraid.

Yeah, I'm sorry too but it had to be done. It was never going to work, not really.

What happened?

I don't know. Nothing much really…

I met her a month ago. It was one of those. I caught her eye at a bus stop and thought 'why not?' got to be worth a go. Turns out it was. I asked her where she was going and within a week we were on holiday together, in Spain.

I know! I know! And I'm not kidding you, it was perfect. Right on the coast of Andalucia, small place, mainly locals. Self catering as well. That's right. Oh yeah. Saffron, shellfish, plenty plenty rioja, plenty plenty beans. And you know what I'm like about me wine and me beans.

I got loads of scribbling done as well. She loves that I'm a writer. Can't get enough of it. What's more, she knows it's a difficult gig and she's really supportive, really encouraging. I'm going to dedicate my first novel to her. It's the least I can do.

Yeah. Well we have an arrangement. She's just started this new job and she hasn't got any time to cook or go shopping, so I do all that and write, while she's out at work.

I think we just didn't give ourselves a chance. We rushed into things. You do sometimes, don't you? And he was that sort of fella. Do you remember, when we got back from Spain, we moved in together straight away, just like that.

I mean don't get me wrong, it was really good at the start. Well it is, isn't it? He was just so into it, into us and, well, everything really. So full of energy. So up, do you know what I mean? And yeah, of course, he had a way with words. You know he wanted to be a writer?

Yeah, I think that was part of the problem, he was a bit of a dreamer. I tried to get him to find some part-time work but he had this romantic idea of what writing was all about, you know? and no idea about how he was going to live while he wrote.

Not that I had a problem with that at the beginning. I mean I don't know if you remember but when we got back from Spain I started that new job and it was really exhausting.

So it isn't just about the sex and the, you know, whatever chemicals I've got in my head at the moment, we complement each other too, we're just so comfortable with each other.

What's that? No, no. No, not like *that*,

in a really really good way. There was one day I remember, when we were away, you wouldn't believe it.

It was the day before we were due to fly home. Oh, mate, special doesn't cover it. I was cooking up a big pot of those fat white beans with some shellfish, trying to make something a bit extra nice, you know, for our last day. But the thing was, it was stupidly hot – the air con wasn't working – and there was something wrong with the plumbing. So the background to this special occasion was this faint – but distinctive – smell of sewage.

I know! It was pretty horrible, I mean pretty disgusting. But perfect too, I mean I can't describe how perfect it was.

Most days, by the time I got home, I was just wiped, so it was good that he was around. I needed a bit of tlc. The problem was going from what it was like in Spain… to that…

Yeah, just like that. Just stuck in a routine.

I remember the exact moment when I realised it wasn't going to work, actually. When I saw there was no future in it

I'd just got back from work one day and I was really tired. I was sitting on the sofa eating my tea. I remember it was chips and beans. He'd cooked and then gone back to the computer room to do some writing. I could hear him, bashing away, and I was just sitting there, on my own, trying to find something to watch on telly, and I found this film about this middle-aged couple falling in love and although it was cheesy, it was sort of nice, you know?

but for some stupid reason it upset me, us being in different rooms. It didn't seem right. I mean I know I

I'd be shouting from the kitchen 'what's Spanish for prawns?' – and she'd be on the balcony giving it 'never mind that, what's Spanish for 'we'd like for you to come and sort the plumbing?" Just silly stuff really,

but that was the point. It didn't matter. The heat, the faintly pervasive smell of shit. None of it. There was nothing that either of us would have changed, not for a minute. Do you know what I mean? It was one of those moments. The whole day was one of those moments. And the thing was, we both knew it. We both understood what it meant, without actually saying it.

And that's what love is, isn't it? It isn't the doing things. It's that understanding, it's those times when you're doing nothing, just sitting there, being together

in an apartment on a hill on the edge of the desert, overlooking the sea, listening to this tiny radio playing some fucked-up casbah shit from across the water

may have overreacted. And I shouldn't have allowed myself to get so carried away by how it was at the start, but you do sometimes, don't you? And I hadn't thought it was going to turn out like that so soon.

I suppose I was just annoyed that he was taking me for granted. Well, taking us for granted actually. It was as though he thought that because we were both so into it at the start, it was all just going to work, that neither of us had to try. It was like he thought there was nothing more to find out about us and he could just sit around, doing nothing,

wasting our time together. What's that? Yeah, it is sad. Because it could have been good, really it could. We could have made something out of it. Even living here.

Anyway. I told him I thought we needed to have a bit of a chat and he said 'I'm just going to fetch some wine' and when I said I couldn't have any because I had work in Morocco or wherever. Having sex or playing cards. Or cooking and eating. The little things. And the wine, of course. Haha! Yeah, you know me. I won't deny that wine plays its part.

That's another great thing about her as it goes. She likes a drink. She can hold it too, which is nice. And I tell you what, she's got this sense of humour that starts off dry and gets drier the more she has. I mean you probably had to be there, but do you know what she said at the end of this perfect day? At the end of a week of love and beans?

'I hate beans. Did I ever tell you that?' And the timing was immaculate, honestly, it was almost surreal,

you know, I couldn't make-up a line like that,

and I was just thinking 'is this really happening? Is this really us?' And it was.

I know! I know! This is me we're talking about. I'll tell you what, though,

the next day and I didn't want to risk it, he said he was going anyway, which sort of pissed me off, because you know me, I like the odd glass. And I thought that was a bit much so

I asked him if he was alright. That was all. And he said 'what do you mean? Is this because I want a drink? Or because I don't want to spend another evening sitting here watching television?' So I just said 'look, I've had a shitty day. I'm tired.' So he said 'I know, I cooked your tea for you didn't I?' And I just lost it. I said to him

'And did you call a plumber?' - because the dishwasher had gone and I'd been asking him to call a plumber for weeks –

or have you been too busy 'writing'?'

So what does he do? He storms off and spends the night in the pub.

By then I'd had enough. It was the sort of row you can get over, but then again

I'm going to be interested to see what's coming next. Because I've got a feeling, you see,

that this is it, this is us,

and that's all there is to it.

Anyway.

That's enough from me.

Oh haha. I love you too!

OK. Next time.

Bye!

sometimes when it's gone, it's just gone and that's the end of it. Do you know what I mean?

There's no going back

It's over.

Anyway.

I'm sorry to go on.

Thanks for listening.

I know. I'll be in touch.

By... yes...yes...OK...bye. Bye.

OPEN WINDOWS

Debz Hobbs-Wyatt

All children except one grow up.

– J.M Barrie

We change the world just by being here.

Your words; but not scribbled on the Post-it notes that cling to everything in your bedroom, fluttering like yellow butterflies.

Nor are they the words posted on Facebook or Twitter or that blog of yours, a testament to a life that, for all its restraints, had more freedom than ours.

And nor are they the words sprayed in electric blue on a sea wall.

No.

These are the words that hang unspoken on our brandy-coated lips as we reach for our coats. These are the words that pound in time to our heavy footsteps as we march from your nan's to the seafront. And these are the words that rattle like dice and when they settle form other words like: how can you be gone, yet be everywhere?

But it's not these words we remember now as we pull our coats tighter, braced against the chill of the sea air.

No.

The words we remember now are the very first ones.

I remember you shaking that can of spray paint; the clicking, the rattling. I remember the smell; aromatic, intoxicating. I remember the hiss as you reached up tall (no wheelchair then) and staked your claim on a tiny corner of this island; on the side of that old café, while we all looked on hoping no one would see.

Those first words are long gone – faded by sea air and then painted over when the café was refurbished. Yet somehow they remain.

Over time you refined the lettering, more artistic, the D in your name enlarged, reversed like a mirror image, your trademark (stolen from your hero and namesake – *Adam Ant*). I remember you scribbling it over and over, trying to perfect it, because you said everyone needs a unique signature. I did try to tell you you needed to invent your own then; not copy *the Ant*.

But thing is, it was you. It *is* you.

Only you.

As we turn the corner the lights on the oil refinery look like the New York skyline (if you squint) and I know we will all look for that signature on the wall and remember those first words we watched you write, thinking we were so grown up, about to start at the big school. Terrified of being caught.

Those first words might have gone but they speak the loudest of all.

Adam woz 'ere.

Tracy, in a skirt far too short, and the heels of her boots far too high, stumbles and reaches for Dave's arm, telling him, 'Don't get any ideas.' All he manages is a grunt. It seems a grunt is all he's managed for most of the day. At one point I saw him bobbing his head in time to 'Prince Charming', dodging the coloured strips of plastic hanging in the backdoor, almost catching them with the end of his cigarette. Those strip blinds are another vestige of the past. It's like time stopped in your nan's bungalow in 1984. I suppose in a way it did. Except for your obsession with social networking, seems like you found a way to stay connected, even when we all moved on.

I wonder what would've happened if there hadn't been an accident, if you'd grown up like the rest of us, mucked everything up like the rest of us.

And then I think maybe it really is better to reach thirteen and get stuck.

We all left, one by one; me to college, Trace to a fella. There was always a fella after she and Dave 'did it' under the steps by the café and we kept watch, you in your wheelchair, remember? God they were at 'it' all the time after that until she dumped him for the ice cream man. Even Dave left eventually for a pokey flat in Basildon, when he got that packing job at the biscuit factory. Your nan says he still works there although it's something else now. She says 'gone are the days of free biscuits' like it's a past she still mourns.

But you – you stayed – in that house, in that moment. Still a kid.

'Nikki,' Trace calls. 'Come on.'

I hear Trace's heels scratching the concrete, her fake tan glows even more orange in the neon of the street lamp. Dave's arm is now stuck out like the handle of a teacup. There's a Morrisons carrier bag hanging off his wrist that bangs against his leg as he walks. 'Let's link,' he says.

It reminds me of us back then: walking arm in arm along the sea front like a chain that could never be broken – the world there for the taking. I wonder as I reach for Dave's arm if we've really changed that much. I mean we're all the same people, aren't we? Trace with the same bleached hair, same pouty lips, only now with filler – it's a wonder she can move them at all. Me fatter, Dave as lanky as ever. His hair has thinned but I guess six kids and three divorces would do that. I reckon whatever Trace taught him that night under the steps unleashed some kind of beast. But we are still who we were, aren't we?

Your nan made me laugh this afternoon when she said Dave looked like a white Stevie Wonder standing there with those strip blinds hanging either side of his face and the way his head bopped in time to Culture Club. At one point his whole body was jerking so much he looked like *he* was the one who had the fits. You should've seen him doing 'Baggy Trousers' when Madness came on. Or maybe you did, eh?

That's what Tracy thinks.

WAG of the year (even if the footballer she married only plays for Southend United – *reserves*) says she's a part-time medium but I reckon the only spirits she talked to today were the ones she found at the bottom of a glass. That's if Cinzano counts as a spirit. I didn't know you could still get it.

'How's that work?' Dave'd said as we filed into the crematorium earlier, 'Part time? You a Medium in the morning and a Large in the afternoon?'

'Sod off!' Trace said. 'Not dress sizes! I talk to dead people. It's my new hobby.'

She couldn't just collect stamps?

'Jesus,' Dave said.

'Jesus hasn't come through yet.'

'No?'

'I did think I was channelling Buddha once, only it turned out it was that bloke who used to work in the bakers, looked like Fred Elliot from Corrie, remember him? Bald head, big jowls.'

All I did was fumble with the order of service and stare at the photograph of you, thinking of all those invites I'd cancelled: Christmas, your nan's eightieth, the *Big Brother* final. Though God knows why you loved that so much, full of freaks; or maybe that was the appeal. You saw good in everyone, even when no one else did. We all grew up and realised people aren't as nice as we think they are – but you, you still believed in pixie dust.

Your nan said you were still inventing those superhero characters, scribbling them on Post-it notes; not on the sea wall any more. And she said you used to write my name.

'People wash 'em off the wall,' she said, 'they're all gone now.' But all I could think was: you wrote my name? But then she had her fingers bent over mine and she looked right at me when she said, 'He hated it when they washed his drawings away. It's like they erased him. Bit by bit.'

So there we were with our 'adult' lives maybe secretly wishing for some of that pixie dust, saying, yeah, sure, we'll come and see you, then one by one the excuses – car trouble, got to work, can't get a babysitter …

But we're here now. That must count. Only as I think that and feel Dave's arm against mine and as the glass bottles in that carrier bag clink together, with each beat, each clink, each footstep, that guilt we all feel digs in even deeper.

'I got plenty to ask that Jesus one,' Trace'd said while I sat on that hard wooden pew and scrunched a tissue to nothing, wondering why more people hadn't made the effort to come. And then wondering what *I'd* ask Jesus. Why he took you so young – forty-three's no age. Why we had to have that stupid argument that day. And why you still wrote my name.

Dave nudged me with his elbow, said to Trace, 'So what would you ask Jesus, eh? Something deep and meaningful about the universe?'

'Yeah,' she said, 'I'll ask him if that *Da Vinci Code* is true.' I heard Dave snigger and watched Trace thumb through the order of service and stop at your face. 'That Tom Hanks is fit.' *Tom Hanks?* 'Poor love, never was destined for a normal life was he? Not after what 'appened.'

'Tom Hanks?' Dave said.

'No – Adam – you doughnut.'

'No' is all we could muster.

'I thought I'd see his mum here,' Trace said.

'She died when he was a kid,' I said.

'I know. Thought his dad might come too, although no one knows if he's dead or not.'

'Maybe he'll shows up with Jesus,' Dave said. He sniggered again, but it quickly turned into a grunt and he didn't say much after that.

That's when I found myself staring at the front as the vicar whispered something to your nan and that new bloke of hers, and then they started playing the Flying Pickets, 'Only You'. It was number one that Christmas. It seemed to be playing everywhere we went while you were in the hospital. All you kept saying was 'Don't worry, we're all going to be okay.' It was like the part of your brain for negative thoughts was the part that got damaged.

I rooted for another tissue and felt Trace lean in and all I could think was: *Don't say anything. Don't bloody say anything.* I expected some quip about whether you and me ever did 'do it' (at thirteen? Come on …) and what really happened that morning after New Year's to make you leave in a huff. But that's not what she said. Her arm brushed mine just as the Flying Pickets sang the words, 'It's just the touch of your hand' and she whispered, 'Adam's here. Standing right by that coffin. He still loves you.'

'Sod off,' I said.

We walk to the top of the bank, a slope of concrete squares held together by tufts of weed and dribbles of black tar. The tide's halfway out. The sea mist seeps into everything. Used to make our chips soggy, remember? Your nan said you always wanted to be in the Royal Navy, if you hadn't – well, *you know*. She lowers her voice when she says the words 'got run over', even after all these years, like if she says it softly it won't hurt. You always told *me* you wanted to be a Storm Trooper, before you wanted to be Superman. She thinks you always left windows open to smell the sea. Even if it is only the Thames estuary and it stinks. But I know the real reason.

'Used to tell 'im he'd catch his death,' she said.

'Don't be daft, you can't catch it,' you'd said.

But looks like you did; pneumonia and the rest.

I'd watched her pull back the curtains in your bedroom to show me the Post-its. She said at the end you had to be in the dark, the light brought on the fits. Then she handed me a Duran Duran tape and said, 'Put that on for me, Love.'

'Yeah,' I said, but all I could think was I'd not seen a tape recorder for years.

Or listened to Duran Duran.

Or said what I'd never been able to.

Next thing your nan was shoving a tissue into my hand saying, 'Let it all out, Love,' pulling me to her bosom and choking me with that *Charlie* perfume I can't believe she still wears. And then she said, 'But don't let your tears drip on that tape cassette.'

We stand in a line and look at the flashing lights in windows over in Kent.

'He loved Christmas,' I whisper and I feel Dave lean into me.

'He told his nan he wanted one more,' Dave said, 'shame. Fancy dying on your birthday.'

'His nan said it's better we remember 'im the way he was,' Trace says.

I wonder if she means before the accident.

I remember that morning, the first day of 1984, your nan rang to ask where you were, why you weren't back yet. And I said, but you left ages ago. You decided to walk.

I didn't tell her why.

And later when we went to look for you someone said a boy had been knocked over up by the Gold Mine Night Club. It was the first time I knew critical meant something else and not just a word Mum used about me – you can't wear *ra-ra* skirts for school, Nicola. Your tie's too thin, Nicola.

Shoes not bomber boots, Nicola. I know as we sit here now we're all thinking about those weeks we thought you were going to die, when 'Only You' was number one. And you insisted, even then, we were all going to be okay.

Didn't stop the guilt though; we all took part of the blame; shared it out – your nan, Dave, Trace. Even my dad because he said he was supposed to be driving you home. But I took the biggest slice. And the worst part was you never remembered the argument. Or if you did, you never said. And now all I can think about is what your nan said today, about you writing my name. I saw it on some of those Post-its. I had to look away.

'I said I'd come loads of times,' Trace says looking down at her patent leather boots, as if she can catch her reflection in the shine. Maybe she can. 'But you know how it is. His nan told me he really wanted to get us all back together. Why didn't he just tell us?'

'He did,' I say. 'What do you think all those Facebook invites were about?'

'Yeah,' Dave says. 'I always accepted 'em.'

'Me too,' Trace says. 'Never went.'

'I usually sent my virtual self,' Dave says. 'He's better looking.'

We all laugh and I don't mean soft sniggers but great big whoops that seem to echo off the sea wall and then Dave says, 'His nan said he always felt connected to us, because of Facebook,' and then he starts to cry. He wipes his nose, smearing snot across his cheek. It sits there glistening and I want to tell him it's gross – but I don't.

'I know I should've come,' Trace says. 'I meant to – but what with Kev, you know, the footie season. And Olly, he's fourteen now, needs running about and—'

'It's too easy to make excuses,' I say. 'Like how hard is it to find a window?'

'Ooh, get you,' Dave says. '*Find a window*. You always were the posh one. Working for that fancy bank. Not many bloody windows in a factory.'

He laughs again then he unlinks arms so he can set the carrier bag down.

'I read his blog every day,' Trace says and I see Dave turn his head towards her. 'Really?'

'Right up to the very end, just before his birthday.' She looks away as she speaks.

'So what was the last thing he said?' Dave says.

She picks at the zipper on her Burberry coat.

'Well?'

When she still doesn't answer Dave says, 'His nan said he stopped in the summer.'

'Oh.'

'She said he'd run out of things to say, that's when she knew. He even stopped posting notes all over his room, ideas about where he wanted to go or what he wanted to do. Superheroes he wanted to draw. He told her he felt like everything was shutting down, like all them shops on Canvey High Street.'

We laugh again.

'So he knew?' Trace says.

'S'pose.'

'Okay, I didn't read his blog but I always meant to.'

'Me too,' Dave says.

'Like we all *mean* to do things,' I say.

'Yeah.'

'It was like a kid's blog,' I say. 'About his favourite eighties bands, loads of his art, superhero stuff. It's all still there. We can all still read it. It can't be washed away.'

'Yeah,' they say.

'He even wrote a poem for Christopher Reeve when he died.'

'No?' Trace says.

'No?' Dave says.

'Yeah,' I say. 'About flying. He always told me he wondered what it would feel like to fly.'

'Maybe he is now,' Dave says.

'Yeah,' we say.

Now we don't know what to say, so all we do is stare at the sea, black, cold, tide feels like it's on its way in until Dave finally says, 'Brave bugger.' We don't know if he means you or Christopher Reeve or both. Maybe it doesn't matter.

'We should sit down,' I say. 'It'll be warmer.' So we lower ourselves onto the lip of the slope, our feet dangling, looking down at the shingled beach. I feel the cold of the concrete against my backside and the sting of the cold air stiffens my cheeks. I think about my empty flat. 'We emailed once in a while,' I whisper. 'Adam was great when I left John. Sent me all these silly games and daft jokes. Boyish things. He just wanted to cheer me up I suppose. Only sometimes …' I stare at the lights, watch a green one blink on and off in the distance.

'Sometimes?' says Dave.

'Sometimes I wish I could've just had one adult conversation with him.'

'What would you say?' Dave says

'The one thing I never did.'

I pull my woollen hat further down over my ears and we link arms again, the sea air sinks in deeper. No wonder your nan said she'd stay indoors – with her seventy-three-year-old toy boy. And now I have an image in my head I really don't want.

'Maybe we could all have been a bit more like Adam,' I say, 'I left John because he was too serious.'

'When was the last time you saw Adam?' Dave says.

'Couple of summers ago,' Trace says.

'You saw him quite a bit didn't you?' Dave says to me.

'Used to.'

'Oh,' he says and now he unlinks again and fumbles in his pocket, then cups both hands together and I watch the flame of his lighter bend over until he manages to light his ciggie. I want to tell him not to blow it my direction like I used to when he sneaked fags, what was he, fourteen? But I don't say anything because suddenly what does it matter?

'Sorry,' Trace says.

'For what?'

'You and John. Thought you two were solid. At least there were no kids.'

'That was part of the problem,' I say. I don't tell them about all the years of therapy, of blaming myself for what happened to you. 'Anyway, we can't all be like you and Kev.'

'Yeah,' she says. 'Solid.' She adds, 'I always take him back when he cheats. How solid can you get?'

Dave now swings his head in her direction. 'I might've not been a perfect husband, and they might've all left me in the end but I never cheated. You deserve better than that, Trace.'

'Yeah,' she says.

'You do, Trace. Much better.' He sucks on his cigarette, blows a smoke ring. 'Dunno why you stay.'

'Habit?' she says.

He asks Trace to hold his ciggie and next thing he's lifting a bottle out of the carrier bag and I'm about to tell him I hate lager when I see it's a small green bottle and the label says *Snowball*. You and your nan's favourite. I let the bottle sit there in my gloved hands.

Now he takes his keys from his pocket and holds his hand around mine as he snaps off the lid with a silver opener. 'I get to see my kids every week,' he says. 'Three to fifteen they are now.' Then he turns to Trace to open her bottle and shakes his head when he sees she now has his ciggie in her mouth. She told us she'd given up.

Next thing, we hear kids laughing and behind us the clatter of footsteps. That's when I turn to see four shadows running towards the slope. One looms extra large against the sea wall, a boy – he looks like he's wearing a Santa hat. It jogs a memory loose. You were wearing a Santa hat, it was your thirteenth birthday, three weeks before Christmas, four weeks before the accident. You were holding a sprig of mistletoe, dangling it between us. It was the first time I'd kissed a boy. I thought all kisses were meant to feel like that until I realised you had a mouthful of crackling space dust.

I feel Trace and Dave watching me. Hear the footsteps recede.

'That was us once – so full of life, all that expectation,' I say.

'What was?'

'Those kids.'

'What kids?'

'And to think you two wanted to get hitched.'

'As if,' Dave says.

'As if,' Trace says handing him back the ciggie.

All I hear now is the wind, the rush of the sea and the whoosh of the traffic on the road. I wonder if you really are here. I wonder if Trace still fancies Dave? I wonder what would've happened if I'd let you kiss me again.

'I used to feel guilty,' I say and now they both turn to look at me. 'Every time I looked at Adam I saw what I'd done. That's why I stopped coming. All I could think about was that day, that stupid fight. If he'd not stormed off, if Dad had given him a lift home …'

'It was an accident,' Trace says.

'I know.'

'It wasn't your fault.'

'That's what all the therapists said.'

'Nicola French in therapy?' Dave says. 'You always seemed so together.'

All I think now is it's been a long time since anyone called me Nicola French. But I guess I'll be getting used to that.

I watch the end of Dave's ciggie bob around like a firefly and then he throws it down onto the beach and takes a swig of Snowball.

'It was the driver's fault,' Dave says. 'Well over the limit. No one blamed you.'

'I know,' I say. 'That made it even worse.' And now all I can see is me at home, Mum whispering to Dad, saying I'd not touched my dinner again.

I let the sweetness of the Snowball coat my tongue, watch Trace lean against Dave. We sit like that for a while, drinks in our hands, listening to the *ding ding ding* of a bell somewhere on the sea. The *clink clink clink* of our bottles as we make a toast to you.

Our breaths curl like genies escaping from a bottle.

'If you could have one wish,' I say, 'what would it be?'

'To be happy,' Trace says. I'm sure Dave winks at her then.

'For Adam to be here now, with us,' he says.

'He is,' Trace says.

'You don't really think that do you?' I say.

'Don't think it, know it,' she says.

Now Dave is looking at me. 'And your wish?'

But all I say is, 'He wanted to go out with me; a New Year's snog and I said no.'

New Year's Eve, 1983. Trace and Dave were playing on the Sinclair Spectrum upstairs and Mum and Dad were in the kitchen. We were on the couch. You'd been acting weird since the kiss. I suppose I always knew it was coming.

'So do you like, wanna be my girlfriend then?' you said and I remember fumbling with a hairclip, pincer-ing it over my finger until it hurt, until you said, 'Well?'

'I don't know,' I said.

'A New Year snog then?'

'Adam, don't spoil it.'

'Can I have a feel of your—?'

'Adam!'

'Dave said it's polite to ask first, I was only—'

'No.'

That's when I saw your face crumple up and you stormed off upstairs to see what Dave and Trace were doing on the Spectrum and then you went to bed and Mum couldn't work out why you didn't stay up to see in 1984. Or why you left before we got up the next morning, a note on the coffee table saying *I decided to walk home. Thanks.*

'Nikki?'

When I look back they're both watching me and Trace says,

'Maybe Adam wasn't the only who got stuck in 1984.' Before I respond she adds, 'He always seemed so happy. Always said we'd all be okay, like it was his motto, his super power. So we have to be, right? For him.'

'Haven't you ever wished you were still a kid?' I say.

I think about something you said to me once. Then I think I don't want to go through puberty again, no way.

'God yeah,' Dave says. Now it's our turn to look at him.

'You still are a kid,' Trace says.

He takes another swig of drink. Gulps it down. 'What d'ya think Adam's wish would be?' he says. 'You think he wanted to grow up?'

'He wants for us to be here, like this together. And not just today, make more of an effort,' Trace says.

'Trace?'

'Yeah, Dave?'

'You don't really talk to dead people do you?'

'I'm still learning. But he is here. We just need to find a way to let him in.'

'Leave the window open,' I mumble. I think about what you told me once. 'You're like my Wendy,' you said.

I didn't know what you meant then.

'Know what we should do?' Dave says and I see him reach into that bag and bring out what I think at first are three more bottles.

As he does I hear those teenagers again, the dash of excited footsteps up the slope, more sniggers and I remember that night, the summer after your accident. 'Hold it like this,' you said pressing the can between my fingers. 'Point and press,' you said. 'Balance on my wheelchair if you want. Write it up high.'

'Nik?'

I turn back.

Dave is holding out a can. 'Over there on the wall. Write something, anything.'

It's the same thing you said to me. But I couldn't do it. I knew what I wanted to write, one word that I could never say.

'Come on.'

Dave and Trace have now stood up and are looking over at the sea wall.

'Don't be a chicken, Nik.'

I scramble to my feet and feel Dave's hand reach for mine.

'Sure you can think of something.'

But I know what to write.

I stand in front of that wall that glows orange in the light. The wall is so much taller than the one they had here when we were kids. I reach up. I shake the can, hear the hiss and breathe in the smell. I don't look to see what they write but I hear Dave say he's trying to write the D like you did. But he laughs and says it looks more like a blob.

So next thing we all stand back and link arms again.

I see what they've written, *Dave woz 'ere*, and *So woz Trace* and under that *18-12-2013* but it seems as if my word, written in electric blue and smaller than theirs is the loudest of all; like a scream. *Sorry.*

Then I lean in again and write *Nikki was here as well*. And Dave says, 'Even your graffiti is posh.' And I say, 'Yeah,' and as we stand here I know they've seen the other word but neither of them say anything.

The street lamp flickers.

Trace looks right at me. 'I know you don't believe me, but if I know Adam, if there's a way back, he'll find it.'

I swear she rolls her eyes like that Snowball has finally tipped her over the edge and she says, 'You know that place between sleep and awake?'

'Yeah …' and now all I can think about is that book, it's what you read to me once. But she doesn't know that, does she?'

That's where I'll always love you. That's where I'll be waiting.

I reach into my pocket for a tissue. But now she's whispering to Dave and I wonder if she even said it, if I just imagined it.

'Can we go now, I'm freezin' me effin' balls off,' Dave says.

Now I know I didn't imagine that. But just like that – the moment breaks, shatters like glass, and I imagine pixie dust floating to the ground to the sounds of our laughter.

We don't leave right away. Dave says we should get together next week, maybe Boxing Day, and before I know it I'm inviting them all to my flat in Leigh. Dave puts the bottles and the spray paint back in the bag and we walk back towards the slope.

That's when I we hear it again.

Running footsteps, only this time I see only one shadow, standing tall, but when I go to say something to the others I know they don't see it. Just as they don't see what's written right there next to the word *sorry* in electric blue, three words.

Adam woz 'ere. The D reversed.

LOOKING FOR THE CASTLE

Elizabeth Baines

You were still miles from home, but the moment of getting there was in your head already, the click of the key in the door, the clang of saucepans from the kitchen, your husband cooking. The sound of things knocking into place. Your life. You put your foot down; the land wheeled, flat as a canvas, a black scribble of petroleum works sliding by in the distance, a contusion of clouds pushing up on the horizon.

And then the sign came up, the name of the town where you lived for two or three years as a child.

You'd never been back, but now the place scraped on your mind: a knot of tanneries and terraced houses in a curve above the wide watery spaces where the Mersey joins the Manchester Ship Canal, surrounded by green country on the other two sides. The moan of boats coming in from the misty Irish sea. The black scar of the terrace you lived in. The boom of your father's Irish voice.

The count-down signs to the sliproad appeared, and though you didn't intend to, you flicked the indicator, and there you were driving back towards the memory: the yard of scorched cinders beside the end-terrace house, the high board fence your father erected to keep away prying eyes, a fag stuck to his lip, his big stiff body bending and stretching, the hammer biting and snapping all day. The way, when you went to call him for his tea, his face in answer was cold and impassive, his mouth a hard line. The way you cringed.

The door he made in the side of the fence, the pain and shame leaking out as you and your sister, escaping, stepped through. The cold feel of her fluffy coat, the way she winced as you took her arm.

The walk down the hill, the road seeming unstable under your feet. The fat woman on her doorstep, arms folded and staring at you frankly; the kids you didn't know sending calls like radar and missiling past. The turn at the bottom where the Bridgewater Canal plunged with the road into the scab-red wall of the tannery, an unlit tunnel hammering with factory sounds and slamming with cars.

You stood steeling yourselves as cars batted past, teetering at the entrance on the narrowest of pavements, hit by your own flapping clothes. In a gap in the traffic you held your breath and grabbed hands, and ran like mad to the other side.

The other side, where the industry ended and another landscape began: a double row of pink semi-detached houses lacing up a steep hill between fields, and at the top an ancient village with a ruined castle, an escape to a fairytale land.

Now, all these years later, you were on a ring road that didn't exist then. You couldn't see the town, it was hidden by curtains of newly planted trees, and you didn't recognise the district names on the signs. At last a name seemed vaguely familiar, though when you turned off, the view opening up had nothing to do with the dark clotted place you'd remembered: ahead, beyond a small park, pale modern industrial roofs tipped away to the river in the distance. But as you turned at the junction you saw the glint of the nearby canal, and a short way along there was a sign with the name of the road where you lived.

The whole area was razed. The factory had gone, the ground where it stood had been landscaped over. No one would know it had ever been there.

*

No one would know. No one did. You set yourself the task of surviving, and you did. You lost that spaced-out feeling, you no longer flinched at sudden movements, your skin no longer shrank back to itself. You even forgot that that was how it was. You stopped thinking about yourself. You were strong, stronger than most others; you stood in front of a class of children and felt them draw from your strength.

And then there was the lover. 'You're such a strong person,' he'd tell you, stroking your shoulder.

*

In this opened-out landscape, the road you'd lived on, which you'd always remembered as steep, was an innocent minor slope. There at the bottom, in place of the grimy terrace where the woman stood staring, a wire fence enclosed a yard of shipping containers in primary colours, washed by silvery weeds. Opposite, where once a high stone wall enclosed the grounds of a big ruined house, a small estate of rosy brick had been built, and, as you watched, a man in a bright blue jumper came out to his car, whistling into the glassy twenty-first-century day.

There was nothing here of your past.

You should have been glad. But you found yourself ambushed by loss.

And when you drove up the road and there was the terrace you lived in still standing, you felt something close to relief.

The bricks were clean now, the doors and windows replaced with white plastic, but there at the side of the end house was the high wooden fence your father once built.

You got out of the car and leaned your hands on the now-grey boards.

You peered through a hole where a knot had dropped away in the years in between. Bright white slammed your eye: a kitchen extension had been built across the yard, blocking the view of the garden beyond. Your vision adjusted. Through windows in the near and far sides, a square of garden was after all still visible. And framed in that bright-green square was a boy, hands in pockets and foot on a ball, the sun making an aura of his bristly hair.

You felt displaced.

It was ridiculous, you thought, you should turn around now, put it all behind you again, get back on the motorway, get home. But then there you were instead, driving over the space where the factory once stood, and up towards the village with the castle.

There were no fields now; to the left an industrial estate patchworked the hill, and a council estate tumbled away on the right. At the top, at the start of the village, nothing, clearly, had altered: there at the start were the four Jacobean houses, giving way to two rows of nineteenth-century cottages that curved off around the crest of the hill. Yet the way it was now was not the way it had been your mind: in your mind it had always been sunk in winter late-afternoon gloom; now, in the spring midday, the houses baked like yeasty loaves, mullioned windows fizzing light.

You parked just a little way into the village. Now, as then, there was no one about. You set off walking, the way you did with your sister all those years before.

You'd walk, you and Eileen, to where the cottages ended at a common, and there you'd stop before setting back again. You'd stand, arm in arm, looking out across the green at a copse in the distance, etched on a reddening sky like a drawing in a fairy-story book. You would shiver. It would be dark soon:

you'd have to get back, you'd be in trouble all over again if you didn't, to the door in the fence, the grind through the cinders, the flinch of the back door opening, the blue swipe as your father looked up from his paper. There was no escape into a fairytale.

Now, all these years later, when you got to the end of the cottages you came up short. Where you'd fully expected the green to open out on the left was a high wall of privet, the roofs of established houses just visible beyond.

You felt uneasy, troubled. You'd spent your life putting it all behind you, but now it felt important, imperative even, to have remembered this correctly, and yet you hadn't.

Now you were somehow desperate to find the common. You decided, disquieted, that it must be further off the main road than you'd remembered. You turned into a side road between more high hedges. The wind dropped; the hidden gardens pooled with birdsong and the private hush of suburbia. You turned a corner: this would it be it, you felt sure. Blocking the way was a red-brick primary school, and beyond it a thick wood of sycamores, their tops swaying in the high-up wind.

This couldn't be it at all. Your sense of loss increased.

As you reached the main road again you spotted the sign you missed when you turned in: *The Common*.

It *was* the place after all. You understood now: the green had been built on long ago, not long, probably, after you left the town, the copse, black and still and distant and enchanted in your memory, become those tossing schoolyard trees.

You felt relieved again, vindicated. But also once again negated by the change. And seized by a sense of something important almost grasped but out of reach, something that needed to be retrieved.

*

There was a time once before when you had the urge to resurrect the memory. You wanted to tell the lover, you thought of it, had the urge. But you didn't, you thought better. You didn't want to make it a truth about you for him, since by then it wasn't the truth about you at all. But when, as he reached for his cigarettes, you noticed his scar, caught sight of the knife-kiss of silver on his inside wrist, and he saw you seeing, well then he told you – desperate, grateful to tell you – all the things he had suffered. He wanted you to know that that *was* the real truth about him.

He sat frozen, his face a mask as he remembered. You felt disturbed. The light in the room angled downwards and the shadows purpled.

But you thought: you were lucky, luckier than him. You'd put your past pain behind you in a way that he hadn't, and it had made you strong.

*

Now, once more on the main road of the village, it came to you with a thud that you hadn't seen the castle.

How could that be? The way you remembered, it was unmissable, lowering and huge on a stony outcrop above the road.

It must be further on… But no, you were sure that this was as far as you and Eileen ever came…

In the buffeting wind, you felt dizzy.

You opened up the map you'd brought from the car, and found the road, coloured yellow. Yes, there was the castle, marked in gothic lettering, further on, in fact right at the far end of the road. You *must*, after all, have walked further than the common all those years ago. It seemed urgent now, somehow, that the details of the memory be accurate, yet here was the whole of it in doubt.

The wind flung your hair, flapped the map. You set off for the far end of the village. The gusts knocked you, sometimes against you, sometimes pushing you on. You felt disconnected, with the ground, with the surroundings, thirties semis you didn't remember set back behind long front gardens. Two teenage lads overtook you on skateboards, gliding with ease through the village and the twentieth-first-century day.

You reached the end of the road. You remembered none of it.

The area here, though, had recently been redeveloped, with a small new roundabout and two new roads, one curving off left around the far side of the hill, the other leading right into a bijou housing estate. Ahead was a landscaped walkway to the council houses pouring off down the hill.

Could the changes have brought the road further away from the castle? Could it be hidden behind the new buildings?

But surely it was more imposing than that...

A patrol car stopped beside you, a friendly young cop winding down his window and asking if you were lost. You'd passed the castle, he told you. You insisted that you hadn't and he looked at the map and agreed you were right, it should be right here.

'What's that back there, then?' he asked, pointing the way you'd both come.

You peered at the map, which showed a ruined priory near the start of the village, set well back off the road. 'That's a priory,' you told him.

Why were you looking for the castle? he asked, and you told him, that as children you and your sister walked up from the town.

He cracked a laugh of surprise. 'You walked up through the estate?! Even *I* wouldn't walk up there!' He was very young, he couldn't imagine a time when the council estate with all its problems wasn't there.

The two feisty girls of his imagination, unfazed by the neighbourhood louts, rose up to replace your cowering, shivering selves.

And you felt effaced.

*

You'd felt that before.

When the lover reached for his cigarettes, he had a way of doing it, dropping his arm in a curve, that made you think of someone drowning. He would light up and breathe, and his eyes would bruise sideways out of the present into the past.

In the beginning it was all you wanted, to rescue him from his past.

But you started to resent the way he gave you no option, the way, whenever he said you were strong, his mouth would then close in a line, his upper lip coming down like a lid.

*

'Good luck looking for the castle!' The policeman moved off.

The two skateboarding lads, coming back, stopped and kicked up their boards and, eager to help, asked if you were doing a survey. You saw yourself as they saw you, the kind of woman who'd be doing a survey, detached casual observer in leather jacket and jeans, someone in control. The image floated, disconnected from you.

'Trip down memory lane,' you told them, feeling fraudulent.

*

When you said you couldn't go on, the lover went still. You touched his arm, but he didn't move. He didn't speak. His face was expressionless, his mouth an unyielding line. You even thought he might hit you.

Later you wondered. A man like your father: how could you ever have got involved?

*

'Are you lost?'

A round face with wire specs popped up from behind a low garden wall, and a stout man who'd been weeding unseen got to his feet.

You laid the map on the wall, and you and he looked at it together.

He scratched his head. Like the policeman, he'd thought the priory was a castle, and, though it was clearly marked on the map, he didn't know of any other castle just here. It must, he said, be a pretty inconspicuous ruin.

Could it be that you *invented* the castle of your memory?

Imagined, *dreamt* your own past?

The wind grabbed the map, you had to secure it with your hand.

The man stood thinking, hands on hips, stomach swelling in a grease-marked sweater. 'There's lots of ruins in this area, though,' he said. 'Lots of history.'

His glasses blinked. All around the bright day glittered.

'Tell you what,' he said, 'I've got a friend who's a local historian. If anyone can tell you, he can. Come on in and I'll get you his email.'

You opened your mouth. You wanted to say that it wasn't that kind of history you were interested in; but you didn't want to, either, you couldn't. You couldn't tell the truth, that you were looking for a memory. It wasn't a memory people could believe, it didn't seem right, it didn't seem seemly, and you weren't even sure any more if you believed it yourself.

You followed him down the path as he waved at his weedy garden explaining that now he'd been made redundant he had time to tackle it at last. He led you round to the back of the house and a green space surrounded by tall trees.

Here there were hens, running free.

And you thought of the hens your mother kept at the bottom of the garden in the town down below.

They were his wife's hens, the man was telling you.

They strolled, lifting their legs with their measured clockwork motion, making their sound like a spring uncoiling.

The man led you up the steps and through the back door to a narrow untidy kitchen.

You waited while he scrabbled between unwashed dishes through sifts of paper.

Leaf shadows simmered up and down the walls, trembled on the clutter.

There was something, some truth, still out of reach but bubbling upwards now...

Behind you, triumphant, the man had found his friend's email. He wrote it down then led you out, past the hens and back down the long front garden to the gate. He said, 'Let's check the map again.'

You just wanted to go, to be alone, but you played along, you let him help you open out the map and pin it on the wall.

He gave a cry. He was pointing to the yellow line you thought you'd been following. 'This isn't the road!'

It was the bus route, he told you, approaching the village from the other side of the hill, and ending where the village road began. You understood now: the castle, after all, was at the start of the village; you'd driven past it before you parked, where, close and high up, it would be out of view from inside the car.

The map billowed, as if shrugging something off.

*

There was another fence your father erected: a high wire one for the hen run. He stood on steps fixing the wire, whistling with a sound like a faraway wind.

You went out to the hen run to call him for his tea. He had stopped whistling. He was leaning on one of the posts. He didn't see you approach. He looked up and saw you, and wiped his expression. But you'd seen it already: a faraway, helpless expression. A look of longing and loss. A look like a bruise.

*

'Which road did you live on?' the man wanted to know, and when you told him he cried, 'So did I!'

He folded up the map and handed it back. 'Know where you are now?'

You nodded, thinking of what he must have been like as a boy: confident, pleasant, a little plump perhaps. Perhaps, as you and your sister made your timid way down the hill, he was one of the children running past...

Something happened to your memory. It widened, warmed: hot sun slid down the red-brick tannery wall, spilled onto the terraces, turning them russet, and spread in a glow over the town, melting it into the present.

B

John D Rutter

It all started with a tweet. I was aware how things can escalate, but I'd no idea it would get as big as it did. It's certainly not fair what happened to me regardless of what you think of him. And it's not like I named names.

It was one of those idle Tuesday afternoons, when you're sort of working but not paying attention, you know, browsing at the same time. I was editing a story about a piano tuner and there was a lot of news on the Internet about this talent show versus that talent show, who's going to appear in the next series, who'd had a tiff with Simon Cowell, that sort of stuff. And I remembered Phil, Phil the Piano I used to call him, my piano teacher when I still had aspirations about things like that. I wondered how he'd take all of this Jimmy Saville-Dave Lee Travis-Stuart Hall speculation. Anyway it was about ten years ago when Phil used to tell me his showbiz gossip when he was working at the BBC. Phil was gay, said he knew a secret. A big secret.

So there I was at the laptop thinking about stories and I just tweeted to see what would happen. 140 characters, I have this rule where I try and use all 140. This is what I tweeted:

You think they've caught them all? Saville, DLT, Rolf, Stuart Hall. I've got news. THE BIGGEST fish is yet to be exposed. Watch this space…

It was just a throwaway. I was only trying to build up my own following. You know that old adage, no such thing as bad publicity. It's hard being a literary critic, occasional journalist and barely-read blogger.

I got *hundreds* of replies, lots of them guesses. I made a point of replying to as many as I could, "No" or "Nope" (admittedly breaking my own 140 character rule but you have to flexible.) That just led to more hits. I'd been tweeting for about six months when I'd tweeted that first tweet; I was following about 300 people and I had about 150 followers. Within three or four days I was past 1,000. Then people started re-tweeting and it started trending and went up to 5,000. In the end I got scared it was all getting out of hand. I tweeted again (using the full 140):

Thanks for all the tweets about the Big Fish. You can stop guessing now. I'm not going to reveal who he is. I have to protect my sources.

It seemed to calm down for a few days after that. I'll admit it did help having a bigger following when I had a couple of reviews published. Then it came to my monthly beer night in Lancaster with Dougie, a tradition we'd kept up since university. He amuses me with his far-fetched stories (he's a professional Geordie and amateur writer) but this particular night he was insistent about the whole tweet thing.

'So, you're telling me you know who the big fish is and you've a witness that was there at the time like?'

'That's what I was told.'

'That's evidence that is. You've got to report him. I mean, what if it's true? You've got a moral duty.'

'What if it isn't true?'

'I thought you said it was.'

'No, I said I knew a guy who speculated about it before all this stuff came out about Jimmy Saville.'

'It's your round.'

'Same?'

At the bar my mind wandered. I didn't agree with Dougie's assessment of the barmaid – too big for my taste. I thought of a video I'd watched earlier on the internet involving two Thai girls. I tried to count the beer mats in frames on the wall instead.

'Five forty.'

I gave her six pound coins and a grin; I always seem to break a note with each round till I end with a pocket full of them. 'Keep the change.'

'You must be feeling flush,' she said. 'Made your first million have you?'

'Not yet, this time next year…'

Dougie and I often speculated about who was going to write the bestseller, be first on TV, write that Oscar-winning screenplay.

'Anyway, I reckon you've got to put it out there,' he said.

'It's not fair if I name him and it turns out he's innocent.'

'If he's innocent, he'll be exonerated.'

'Ruined that guy off Coronation Street.'

'Don't watch it.'

'No, but you see the news from time to time.'

'Well, he was a piss-head anyway.'

'What about my reputation?'

'What reputation? This can only do you good.'

'How come?'

'Well, think of the coverage. How many of that book have they sold, the one where you wrote the foreword?'

'Dunno, few hundred I think.'

'So how helpful would it be to your career if your name was associated with front page news?'

I tried to calculate some numbers while he smiled.

'What if the police come and interrogate me?'

'This is the BBC we're talking about, not the Gestapo.'

'What if I'm wrong and I get sued?'

'Then that's your next story. Sell *that* to the papers an' all. Remember, you'll be a famous writer by then. *Controversial* author…' That made me smile.

'But what if they investigate me?'

'Set up a new twitter account.'

'They can trace that can't they?'

'Who are *they*? The state-controlled-media-police? GCHQ? The FBI? You've seen too many fillams.'

'There's only one syllable in *film*.'

'Beg your pardon, Mr Critic.'

We sat quietly for a moment. Here in the Gaunt I felt safe. Of course I was being paranoid.

'Anyway, never mind the Daily Mail, you've *got* to tell me.' Dougie pointed a stubby finger at me.

'Why's that again?'

'Because we share every secret. It's a rule, like.'

'We have rules?'

'I told you about that bird in the office. '

'You told me you had a fantasy! You never even did anything.'

'Same thing.'

'Hardly. By the way have you heard the latest allegations? They're saying Jeremy Beadle had a small hand in it.'

'Ha ha.'

We went on like this for a while but he wouldn't let it lie. In a way, I suppose I wanted to tell someone. You must have had that feeling when you have a big fat delicious secret; you have to tell at least one person. Anyway, eventually I agreed to give him one letter, he can be persuasive, Dougie, when you've had four pints.

'B,' I said.

He smiled and frowned in an exaggerated way all at once.

'B, eh? Alreet, tell me again what your mate said, the piano man,' he asked.

'He just said that when he worked at the studio in London on that show…'

'Which show?'

'You know, that one where they have dancing and live singing and all that.'

'Puts a new meaning on the name of the show…'

'Listen, that's not the point, the point is *B* was all over the dancers, teenage boys.'

'Not girls?'

'No, Phil said he was like one of those fluffer horses, rearing up, horny as hell, skipping and prancing around them he was.'

Dougie smiled and took a gulp of beer.

'I'm serious.'

'Alreet then, way I see it you have a duty to them poor kids.'

'I can't prove he did anything.'

'Doesn't mean he didn't.' He raised his eyebrows. 'And did your fella…Phil was it…get involved himself?'

'No, I don't think Phil was into older guys from the stories he told me, and by then B would have been no spring chicken.'

'How old is he now?'

'Nice try, looking for clues?'

'I'll get it out of you, mate.'

'Besides, Phil would have been in his late twenties, bit old for B's taste. He was a good-looking lad, mind.'

'You're not…?'

'Fuck off.'

'Anyhow, you can't keep calling him "*B*".' He did that infuriating 66 99 thing with his fingers.

'Why not?'

'Cos if you do, I'm going to sit here all night and speculate about every celebrity whose name begins with B till you're sick of it. I'll include all your favourites. Listen…Beckham, he's a B.'

'Not the right age though is he?'

'Alreet, Billy Connelly? Billy Bragg? Billy Idol?'

'I don't like Billy Idol!'

'That's by the by, where was I…Bobby Ball, Bill Bailey, Bill Oddie?' He looked at me with each name pretending to be watching my body language.

I shook my head. 'Bigger.'

'Bobby Robson? Bryan Robson? Bryan Epstein?'

'No.'

'Barry Humphries.'

'Curiouser and curiouser, but nowhere near.'

'Mm, how about Benny Hill…eh?

I shook my head.

'Bruce Dickinson…'

'Is he the one that does those antiques programmes?'

'Nah, you cock. Iron Maiden!'

'Oh, it's not him anyway.'

'Bruce Springsteen.'

'He's American!'

'So's Bill Cosby – he's a B. Who else? Bryan Ferry…?'

'Avalon,' I sang.

'Y'nah, it's almost as if he was in the room. I know… Bob Monkhouse?' He attempted an impersonation with his eyebrows.

'Eh-uh!' I did the noise from the game show as accurately as I could.

The old man sipping a pint on the next table looked over.

'I can do this all night,' Dougie said.

My beer was almost empty and he would have gone on till he got there. I leaned forward.

'You have to promise me on all that is sacred that you will *never* tell a soul.'

'Scout's honour.' He did a thing with his fingers like something out of Star Trek.

'You weren't even in the scouts.'

'Alreet, cross my heart…' He drew a rough cross on his chest with two fingers.

So I told him.

Up to this point nothing had happened; best mate knows a name that someone once speculated about (and I didn't even know whether he was telling the truth.) But by now the idea had hold of me. I don't know why I did what I did next; I suppose I just felt compelled to do it. This time, contrary to my normal rule, I posted a very short tweet. I just typed his first name.

One word. That's all it took. What I didn't know till it was too late was that the forces of fate were about to take over. You see, Dougie was being a bit of an opportunist himself. He knew some guy from work who knew a journalist. Anyway this freelance journalist gave Dougie a few quid to spill the beans. He protested afterwards that he was under duress, but for pity's sake, you don't just cave in! I've known Dougie all our adult lives and we've playfully wound each other up. He told me he did it just to see my reaction. But what a bastard! Selling *my* secret to the press!

What neither of us realised was that me tweeting it and him saying it added up to two sources. I know what you think – journalists don't follow strict ethical rules – but editors like to know a source. Well, their second source, "deep throat" as I now call him, cock-sucker that he is, led to the whole thing blowing up. So that makes it his fault, doesn't it?

But Dougie wasn't the one that got journalists turning up at his house. They came after me, bloody three of them within about an hour. How did they know where I lived? They just drove up my drive, one of them parked on the lawn. That's private property! They wouldn't go away, and I had to hide all evening and I kept thinking about what would happen if they started to investigate my past. Not that I have anything to hide. I mean there are a couple of stories from football trips when I was with Liz that I wouldn't want to be widely known, but they're subject to tour rules.

What are you meant to do when journalists hassle you? Call your lawyer? Not that I had a lawyer, only the firm that dealt with the divorce, this was a bit out of their field. I was a bit scared that night on my own.

Then the police came to see me. I'm not exaggerating, they ripped the house apart. They emptied all the drawers in the office; they took my laptop, the old PC in the spare bedroom and loads of paperwork. I mean boxes and boxes of everything. They opened all the kitchen cupboards, rummaged through my underwear drawer, felt the pockets of my suits and anything with words on it went in a box; bills, manuscripts, letters. No referencing. No labels. They just emptied the house. Property deeds, insurances, pensions, stories, diaries. Even the review I was actually working on. I asked the one that seemed to be in charge whether I was under arrest.

'Not yet,' he said.

Not yet? I should have checked the warrant he waved in my face when they barged in. Bloody four of them there were. But when I started to protest he said something about helping with their enquiries down the station and I decided to shut up. Then I started to think about why they were after me. I bet it's because of his connections, you know with the OBE or Knighthood or whatever he is...was. Now they were going to look at every web site I'd browsed. What if one of those websites had…you know, the *wrong* kind of porn. I've never even thought about anything like *that*. And that's what they'd be looking for isn't it? But I'm sure I was alright. I mean, Google's got to have some safeguards hasn't it?

They were even going to take my mobile but I refused. I mean, that's *mine*. It's private! The one in charge said they could look up my records anyway. Can they do that? The police can't just look at your browsing history!

I spent most of that evening pacing up and down in the garden smoking, rehearsing what I was going to say when I got to the right authority. Then the police turned up again, they said a neighbour had called because they'd seen someone lurking in my garden at 1am. It'll be that nosey bitch at number 37. I was definitely going to go to the papers about police brutality. I'm the one that gave them the information, I'm not a criminal.

That week was really hard work wise. I do work hard. You can still work and have a look at a few pictures as well. There's no law about looking at web sites is there? I had to phone my editor and ask for an extension. Where was I going to get access to a computer? I'd have to go to one of those internet cafés. I should have done that in the first place, made up a name and used a public computer. But then I didn't realise you could commit a crime by tweeting. What happened to freedom of speech? They're all over 18 the girls on those sites, nothing wrong with looking.

All I'd done was to tweet a name, just a first name. Could have been anyone. Just think of all the celebrities with that first name...okay, maybe none quite so long-established, he is top of the page on Google when you type the first three letters.

What would happen if they arrested me? You hear about what happens in prison. What if there was a cover up? Which would be the better solution if you were in charge? One slightly known tweeter is locked up on some trumped-up charge or another huge BBC scandal costing the tax-payer millions, discrediting the BBC and taking up time in the House of Commons. It had only been a few months since Jimmy Saville. They couldn't afford another cock-up of that magnitude. And, as you know, B is one of the few celebs that carries that sort of reputation. Think about it, who's big enough to rival him? Simon Cowell maybe? Even he's been arguing about children being exploited on TV.

Funny thing is I remember Phil telling me about it with absolute conviction.
'You watch,' he said. 'When he dies, it will all come out.' Prophetic, Phil.

When I saw the headlines the next day I realised the magnitude of it. The tabloids really went to town on him. Some of the journalists had done plays on words about that quiz show he used to do. The people that appeared on that show must be embarrassed. The Sun's headlines were in really bad taste. But the ones that were tweeted about most were a picture of a camp teenage boy of about fourteen being chased around with B's grinning face stuck onto someone else's body beneath his catch-phrase in massive letters. And they'd found some really lecherous looking shots of him too. When you look at him closely in the light of what's been going on, you wonder. I mean he does have that look about him…

Then they all came out of the woodwork didn't they? That's when it got out of control, when the *victims* appeared. One or two at first, then the floodgates opened. Within a fortnight there were nearly fifty. Some of the allegations were decades old, some of them were my age. Surely they can't all have been victims. I mean, when did he have time to be on telly so much and why did none of them say anything before? One of them was a lad who committed suicide in 1986; his mum said she never knew the reason but now it all made sense.

I suppose you have to feel a bit sorry for him; I mean bearing in mind the idea of innocent until proved guilty. He entertained generations of families and his life ended in disgrace.

Was it brave of him to end it? Did he have a choice? There were even suggestions of a Princes Di style conspiracy – that he'd been bumped off because of his royal links. You've got to watch out – there's some nonsense on the Internet.

Not a good way to go though, hanging himself in a hotel room. Alone. Disgraced. I felt sick about that. I thought for a long time whether it was guilt that caused him to do it or whether it was just the shame of facing the enquiry and watching his reputation be ruined. He should have been allowed a proper trial.

I got some really nasty emails and tweets, like it was my fault. I even had my own troll. I got some aggressive messages and had to close down that twitter account.

I refused to read the jokes about how he died in the weeks that followed – that's too sick. I even felt a bit sad, another slice of my childhood memories corrupted. I mean, Stuart Hall! They've ruined my memories of Rolf Harris – all those jokes about Jake the Peg and didgeridoos and Two Little Boys. My mum won't even speak about it, the whole family used to watch the progarmmes together in the seventies – everyone did.

But the stories must have been true; there are too many victims, so the way I see it, I've helped a lot of innocent people.

They'll get a fortune from his estate, those families. I suppose that's the name of the game these days, it's all about compensation culture. So in the end no-one suffered did they? Apart from B, and he was, well, you know…

They wouldn't tell me what was going on and whether I'd have to face any charges or be involved in an enquiry. It took them six weeks to return all my papers and they just dumped everything on the front lawn. Then I got a letter saying something about ongoing enquiries and further investigation into web browsing history and that they are allowed to do that in connection with a criminal investigation. What criminal investigation? I hadn't committed a crime and B was dead. They were only after me because people started to hear about me.

I'll admit it did increase my following. Random House have given me an advance on my book; they were alright as long as I said it's fiction, which of course it isn't. Then I was in the papers a few times, and I got to meet Mariella. By the way did you know she did a sex video? You can look it up on YouTube. I think that's what made them come back – the fact that I was starting to get a bit famous. I mean, if it was illegal you wouldn't be able to see it. Anyway I definitely didn't look at *that* kind of pictures. I know those Asian girls look young, but a mate of Dougie's went to Thailand and said they do look very young but they have certificates proving that they're legal.

I eventually forgave Dougie Deep-throat. His book comes out at Christmas. It's that cheap kind of soft porn for women – you know the fifty shades of shit variety. It's meant to be a secret but I might drop some hints on Twitter. He says the porn thing is nothing to worry about; he does it all the time.

Anyway my conscience is clear. All I've done is expose a famous paedophile. There can be no doubt about his guilt, can there? And I haven't done anything wrong. There's nothing wrong in a bit of adult entertainment (as long as it's consenting adults.) Everyone does it. I bet you're going to look up that Mariella video yourself, aren't you? Just type "Mariella sex video" on Google.

THE HARP AND
THE THORN TREE

Amanda Oosthuizen

I dragged the harp along the pavement to the kerb and was edging it down the three inches to the road when I heard a man sigh behind me. I turned; he grinned like a flash of headlights.

The harp teetered on its wheels. I reached to catch it and glimpsed moonlight silvering the leaves of an oak tree behind a wall. I remembered bush nights in South Africa, on the farm. The time I went with Dad to check on a screaming cow, wild dogs tearing its udders, gun shots and yelps, and the only thing to watch was the moon on the thorn tree.

The harp cracked and rang as it hit the ground. The man pulled me. I hit my elbow on the kerb as I fell and saw dust on the knees of his trousers. A matchbox with *I Love Wigan* on it, fresh looking like a buttercup, dropped from his pocket into the gutter.

I struggled, tried to get up but he kicked hard on my thigh with the point of his shoe then the heel. I had on the silver dress I'd worn for the concert. It was new. It had cost me as much as I'd earned that evening. That's my excuse. I can't disguise it. I was worried about the dress. I've had to live with that for twenty years.

'Jan! Jan!' He let me yell it twice before he pressed so hard on my mouth with the palm of his hand that I bit holes in my lips. He bent over me. His head came close. I smelled aftershave, bright like cardamom and a back smell of cabbage.

As he crouched, Jan kicked him on the ear with the heel of her shoe. She was braver than me. The moment he let go, I ran. I left Jan and the harp. I ran, jumping the scattered bits of Jan's flute, until I got to the station.

I waited on the platform. Three trains stopped. I thought of catching each one, but somehow I didn't. I licked the blood from my lips and rode a swing from years back when I thought that the only way to survive was to keep your feet off the ground.

Jan didn't come so I returned to the street corner with the matchbox and found her curled in the gutter. I stroked her hair. It was wet and stank of urine and her dress was ripped down the back. She rested her cheek on my shoulder and I felt her blood warm against my skin. She had a deep cut from lip to ear.

I visited her in hospital with bunches of irises and offered to teach her the harp. She didn't talk much after the attack and after a few weeks, I stopped going. I could never have done enough anyway.

Twenty years later I answer the doorbell. She is hunched in an old waxed jacket, and if it weren't for the scar, I wouldn't have recognised her.

'Sadie?' she says, unsteadied on the doorstep by a blast of wind. 'Let me inside. I need somewhere to stay.' She scratches at her face with both hands. 'I've killed him.'

I watch a herring gull batter its wings against the side wall of the house.

My house is on a cliff edge. It's battered by rain and sea; moisture has seeped into every crevice. The wood is wet; you can carve your name in the skirting boards with a fingernail. Eighty feet below us, the sea pounds against rocks shaped like towering flames. Not a moment passes when I can't hear waves lashing the rocks and the gulls.

It's strange how some people wear their worst clothes in an emergency. I dress up. Jan digs into the pockets of her jacket and her face is creased like the wax.

'You surprised me,' I say, trying to stretch time. 'How are you?' I smile and step aside to let her in but she doesn't move.

'Did you hear what I said?'

'Yes,' I say. 'Yes.' Because I am absolutely sure. This is what I've been waiting for.

With her head down, she steps inside and hurries towards the kitchen and sits at the table. Her hands reach to her face, pressing against her nose and holding her chin as if she wants to move her features around. Then she strokes her cheeks comfortingly along the line of the scar that stretches from lip to ear like a crack. I take out a bottle of wine and begin to wind in the corkscrew.

'Who is it?' Eddie shouts from upstairs.

'Don't worry.' I call back. 'Go to sleep.'

Eddie could write all he knows about me in an autograph book. He doesn't ask questions. That's what I like about Eddie. He has his own picture of me and it seems to suit him.

I react like a muted trumpet. It's not in my interest to shout and send shock currents. When I was eight my Dad was eaten. It was then that I started to swing on the thorn tree in the back yard. I didn't see what was left of his body, perhaps a hand, probably the head. He had a nice head with speech mark creases at the corners of his lips where he smiled a lot - a nice head though it never said much. He worked in the Kruger Park for a while as a guide. That night he'd got a puncture at dusk. They found the car trampled. Kicked in and stamped by elephants, they said. He must have run. They said it was a leopard that ate him. I remember a small coffin. I was ten and it was smaller than me. When I asked Mum about it, her face looked like one of the rocks they put on top of the grave. I always thought she was going to throw something at me after that.

I put Jan in the roof room.

'You can hear the waves at night. It's a comfort.' I say but it's not. I just don't want her near the children.

When she goes to bed, I play the harp with the window open. I play Welsh songs. The wind blows spray into the house and then it harnesses notes as they shiver in the air and drives the music out to sea. That's my contribution to the world, insubstantial to say the least.

Tonight, I dream a recurring nightmare. I dream of a tanker breaking up and spilling its oil. I'm alone on a raft. I gather up the flailing gulls. I gather so many that the raft lurches as they flap and trample each other. They fight and shriek and peck at the knots that fasten the wood. I shoo them off but they ignore me and the raft starts to dismantle and sink. The faster I shove the gulls, the faster the raft drops.

At four o'clock I wake because I hear a scream from the roof room. I ignore it. I was brought up with screams in the other room. After Dad was eaten, Mum brought cousin Loutjie over to the farm. I guessed from his age that he was her cousin not mine. He slept in a shack in the yard.

Loutjie haunted the farm. He was so still you didn't know you were in the same room as him. He always wore a baggy T-shirt over shorts, and trainers without socks. Always grey. It was the dust on the farm; it made everything grey.

Loutjie would file his nails in winter evenings, rubbing this way and that like he was carving an ostrich from a tree. And in summer, he built himself a harp out of boxwood and strung it with guitar strings. Mum said he'd had one in the Cape. He played it to the cattle. At night he went to Mum's room. I heard his footsteps. That's when I heard the screams. Mum's screams. I rattled her door but it was locked. The first time, when she woke me up in the morning, I said, 'You OK?'

'What do you mean?' she said, and patted her hair like she was checking her standards were still in place. I didn't bother after that. I just hid my head under the pillow.

One summer, Loutjie taught me to swim in the river where

the cattle drank. We swam naked. At first he watched me from the bank. He jumped in with a splash and held me up as I took my feet off the bottom. I remember his fingers pressing into my breasts and the sun burning my eyelids. It didn't take me long to learn to swim. Afterwards we lay on the sand at the river's edge to dry off and he kissed me on the lips. He felt like smooth wood, golden wood without the bark. And he smelled of honey, honey and pine resin. Not many people look better without their clothes but he did. He didn't speak. I would have hated him if he had. That winter he taught me to play the harp.

Eddie leaves early. I watch TV and listen to the radio for mention of a killing. There's nothing.

The children go to school, I cancel a gig at the Dog and Crook and Jan gets up at midday. She takes a loaf of bread without speaking and turns back up the stairs.

'Will they look for you here?' I shout after her.

'Can't think why they should.' She sits half way up the stairs. 'I caught the train and I walked from the station.'

I say nothing. I don't want to know details. I've spent time enough forgetting details.

After the children go to bed, I practise the harp in order to avoid Eddie. I assume that Jan is in the roof room but as I pass the kitchen window, I see her in the garden, at the end of a block of light from the patio doors. She's standing close to the cliff edge. I feel Eddie's hands on my shoulders. I shudder. He moves away.

'She's a school friend,' I say.

He stands between the cooker and the dishwasher.

'From Joburg. Her name's Catherine. The one who kept snakes. Remember me telling you about her?' I surprise myself.

'No.' He doesn't move. 'Go on.'

'Her boyfriend beat her up.'

'Right.'

He goes out without looking round. I should go with him. Jan looks relaxed where the moonlight stops at the edge of the cliff. Perhaps she intends to jump. Maybe she should. I cross my arms for warmth and go out.

'There's something I meant to say.' I touch her elbow.

She doesn't move even though I touched her, even though she's so near the edge.

'I want to say sorry.'

She snorts. Then she laughs and takes a step back.

'What are you laughing at? I mean it. Really. I shouldn't have left you with him. I should have stayed. We might have overpowered him.'

'What are you talking about?'

'I feel responsible. Guilty. You had such a career ahead of you.' I expected the initial apology to be cathartic but it's not, so I keep going. 'I'm sorry. I should have stayed with you in the hospital.' I feel worse if anything.

'I kill someone and you apologise? Forget it.' She kicks a stone over the cliff.

'How did you find him?' I ask.

'DNA test. There was a matchbox.' She walks back to the house.

She stays in her room for three days. I take up her meals. Eddie goes early to work and comes home late and by the time I join him in bed, he's wrapped tight in the duvet and breathing heavily. I practise what I should say to her:

'I need to make plans.'

'You can't stay here forever.'

'Life has to go on.'

I consider handing her over to the police, making an anonymous phone call. In South Africa we avoided the police.

I notice that cereal boxes disappear leaving the cornflakes and crispies in their opaque bags like collapsing foetal sacs.

Eddie dreams about the future but lives the present. For him the future is a wave about to break. I don't think about the future. It's a deep dark pool. South Africa is a land of the future where they say that single mothers build three bedroom bungalows from breezeblocks and cement. I don't want to go back. It holds too much of my past and if I could obliterate the memories I would, but Eddie's persuaded me to retain my South African passport and it sits in the drawer with its tusks and spears and crazy, flapping secretary bird. And just thinking of it makes my fingers shake.

The next day I watch Eddie through the window. He's early. He leaves his car outside the house. I don't think he can see me. I hear the door open.

'Lucy, Carl. Are you coming?' He doesn't call my name.

'Dad.' A door slams upstairs. Footsteps thunder on the stairs followed by a cold draught. They screech in the garden. Eddie throws a ball to Lucy. She kicks it at Carl and it lands beneath a holly bush. Carl stays rooted to his patch of earth. He doesn't know yet that it's more fun if you join in. Eddie leaps and falls to the ground hugging the ball. The children jump on top of him and a great trench opens up around me. Before long, the ball is back under the holly bush.

'How's your visitor?' Eddie stands by my window.

'I didn't think you knew I was here.'

'Do you want to join in?' He points to the children.

'Not really.' I wish I could. My greyness will spoil their bright colours.

He stares at Lucy and Carl taking turns to bounce the ball and catch it and seems to have forgotten his question.

'I thought I'd take the kids to Paris - see Mickey Mouse,' he says.

'When?'

'Tonight?'

'I can't.'

'I'll take them. They'd be better out of the way.' He glances up at the roof room.

A gull flies over and lands on the rotary washing line. It shrieks as if its guts will spew out. The line rotates and the gull launches into the wind but its wings catch amongst the yellow plastic ropes and for a moment it hangs on the line before dropping to the ground. We ignore it.

When Eddie and the kids have gone, the house seems empty and the wind barely ducks the daffodil heads. I take out a bag of sugar and a tin of condensed milk and try to make fudge. It occurs to me that here is an opportunity to change the bedding. I strip the penguin duvet covers and as I dump them in the laundry basket, I glimpse my harp. It's a perfect time to take it to Bristol to have it re-strung.

'I'll bring back a curry. We'll eat downstairs, tonight,' I shout.

There's no reply.

A gull is standing by the woodpile.

I take the long route without intending to. I pass scrubby set-aside and a half-developed golf course. I nearly slaughter a family of chicks that wander through an open gate into the lane. When I brake, the harp knocks against the back seat.

'OK so I love you. What are you going to do about it?' I said it to Loutjie after he'd pushed me against the cold radiator and lifted my skirt and held my hip bones as if he were holding the safety bar on a fairground roundabout, pushing and pulling like a mouth organ.

And two days later I saw Mum smile at her lace as she threaded needles.

'What's that for?' It wasn't often she made lace.

'Loutjie's going,' she said.

'Going?' It hardly came out of my mouth.

'To be married. She's asked me to make her veil. A real lace veil. She'll be beautiful.'

'Who?' I almost yelped like a hyena but I kept my lips together. And it didn't really matter who.

I park in a multi-storey car park and wheel the harp through the streets. My incompetence astounds me. I should have put a limit on Jan's stay.

On the corner by the shop stands a man in a dirt grey coat.

'Big Issue, madam?' He points his face in my direction and

holds out his magazines. He doesn't look directly at me.

I shake my head.

He flicks ash and turns away.

The shop feels good. It is dark, painted in deep red and crammed with all kinds of instruments from crimson Latin percussion, earth coloured African percussion to hand-made Italian melodeons and cheap Chinese violins. Incomplete phrases lap the air. I could stay, soaking in the sound but I give my instructions quickly, leave the harp and begin to dread what might happen next.

Outside the shop the man faces me, 'Big Issue, madam?'

I shake my head.

'You may have changed your mind while inside.' He speaks in an undertone. I am surprised he noticed. Someone might have noticed Jan.

At first, I drive home fast but as I get nearer, I divert. I drive miles. I pass the Glastonbury mound bursting upwards against the iron grey sky and drive into Bournemouth where soaking shoppers dart amongst the cars.

Finally, I stop for petrol and buy a chicken tikka sandwich and a bottle of cherryade. I eat and drink on a cliff top car park and watch rain and waves slap the pier until I fall asleep.

It's dark when I wake and a parking ticket is stuck to the windscreen. I screw it up and throw it into the footwell and drive to an Indian Takeaway and place an order.

Even as I approach the house, I don't want to go in and face Jan. I park and walk along the cliff path.

The flame rocks are visible as I climb down. A flash of pure white trails from the cliff with a symphonic squawk as thirty or forty gulls try to frighten me off. I cling to the iron handrail as the wind races in gusts, tunnelling up from the gully formed by the rocks. The tide is in. Every crash brings a spray and the spray is lit like sparks by the moonlight.

When I watched Mum work at the lace, I wanted to kill her.

'Who is she?' I asked Loutjie one evening as we played the harp.

I was better than him by then and the school authorities had sent me a proper harp.

'She's from back home,' he said, putting both hands on my knees and pulling them apart.

'Get off.' I yanked away from him.

'Come on now. There's no need for that.'

'But why?'

'She's got a place to stay now. Inherited some land.' He leaned towards me.

'I mean it. I'll scream.'

He laughed.

I grabbed the poker from the fireside and held it above my head.

He backed off.

'You've been in touch then, all this time?'

'Maybe.'

'You didn't say anything.'

'Why should I?'

My arm weakened and the poker sank.

He grabbed my wrist and pushed me to the wall. 'One more time, eh?'

'Leave me alone.'

He pressed against me.

I hit the poker at the mantelpiece. The old clock and some ornaments fell onto the stone hearth. He let go and I punched him on the lip. 'You're finished here. You're dead.'

'You're crazy.' He wiped his mouth.

'You heard.' I slammed the door shut.

I told Mum that night. I told her everything. There was a fire. Loutjie's hut burned down and some of the cattle got burned. The next day we dug a big hole by the thorn tree and shovelled everything in. I got a harp scholarship and came to England and cut myself free. I haven't spoken to Mum since I left. No emails. No phone calls. Nothing. I've sliced her off.

I don't go right down to the shore because the swell is deep and unpredictable. I crouch on one of the rock steps with my back against the cliff. A gull settles a metre away. A gust of wind pushes me off balance. A wave sprays. I slip to one side and the gull lurches at me. As I grab at a rock to regain my footing, the gull pecks my ring finger, grasping it in its beak and clamping shut as I shake it. I slip again. It squeezes across my nail. Its eye shines button black. My foot stumbles as it flaps its wings against my cheek scratching like a gloved hand. I brace myself against the cliff and take a handful of gravel and shower the gull with stones. The finger throbs. When I step away from its nest, the gull flaps into a heap against the cliff. I return to the house. Jan is standing in the porch.

'You OK?' she asks.

'What's it look like?' I hurry into the kitchen.

'I heard a noise.' She follows close behind.

'You're up then?' I say.

She doesn't reply.

I run the hand under the cold tap. It stings so I switch to the hot tap. She peers over my shoulder.

'You can fetch the curry. It's in the car,' I say.

She leaves. I brush feathers and gravel from my jacket. My hand is scratched and my sleeve is torn. It takes some courage to look at the finger, but although the whole of my hand aches and the skin is gnashed, I can move everything. I open the first aid box.

'Let me do that.' Jan dumps the curry on the table.

'No way. Put the oven on if you like. I suppose you know Eddie's left.'

She says nothing.

I dab antiseptic onto the wounds, bandage the finger and finish it off with a plaster. I sit at the table feeling dizzy.

'How did you do it?' I ask.

'I made arrangements, met him in a pub. Went out with him for two years.'

It wasn't what I meant, but I'm glad she answered a different question. I don't want details. This is psychotic enough.

'I wanted to be sure.' She folds her arms and shivers.

'Sure it was him?'

'Sure it was the right thing to do.'

'What are you going to do now?' I ask.

Jan begins to unload the tubs from the brown paper carrier bag and at first she doesn't answer.

'Stay here a while.' She speaks quietly.

'What about the police? Someone will notice. Perhaps you didn't kill him. Perhaps he was just injured.'

'Perhaps I'm just lucky.' She replaces the tub of pilau rice in the bag and walks slowly out of the room. 'And his name was Eli. Married with four kids.' I hear her climb the stairs to the roof room and close the door.

All I've ever wanted were clean breaks. Not lucky breaks. Not interludes. I wanted change to be absolute. No turning back. Black and white. Then and now. I should ask her what she wants from me. But instead, I take the night ferry from Poole to St. Malo and call Eddie on his mobile to find out where they're staying. I use my British passport with its lion and unicorn, all brave and hopeful.

But when Eddie takes my hand and asks me what's happened, I want to cry on his shoulder.

'I was bitten by a gull.'

Eddie returns my hand.

'It's true.'

He gives me a second chance and gently pulls away the bandages. It's a comfort having someone close.

I stay for two nights and become part of Eddie's effect on people. The waiter welcomes us to the breakfast table taking Eddie aside to whisper something and returns with a tray of buttered teacakes.

'For breakfast?' I ask.

Eddie shrugs. 'My French isn't all that good. What can I say?'

In Disneyland, Eddie scoops up Cinderella and waltzes her to the castle to applause from the crowd. I refuse to dance with

Prince Charming, after all I have Eddie.

I leave before them. Eddie decides to rent a cottage for a couple of weeks and stay on with the children.

Back home daylight shines through the house. The sun has dried out the moist wood, and the light and dryness has sent the ugliness back into the cavities between the walls, for once, it's warm inside. I half expect to find Jan gone. As soon as I get in, I knock on her door and she opens it. The room has been re-arranged and boxes are positioned on the floor.

'Come down will you?' I say.

My hair used to be short and dyed blonde and I used to wear heavy make-up, that's why my passport photo looks so unlike me - my South African passport, that is.

I massage the dye into Jan's hair, pressing against her scalp. I'm feeling the bone landscape of a murderer. I try to picture the magical flute player. I imagine the shreds of time we'd had together, the duets we played. After I've dyed her blonde, I take the scissors, trimming close to her ear where the scar ends and pointing into the back of her neck.

'How did you do it?' I can feel the muscles in her neck tense into lumps like seashells as I run the sharp edge near to her eye.

'Do what?'

I found out no more. And when I recall the beginning, I remember that all she ever said about the murder was 'I've killed him.' It's enough to make you laugh, the way it all worked out.

Six months later I receive a letter from South Africa, from Jan. She tells me she's writing with bad news. I glance through but every sentence pulls me up, a small electric shock. She found the farm empty and run down. The locals mistook her for me, so the plan worked and she's taken over where I left off. The bad news, she says, is that Mum died last spring, before she arrived. I hold my breath. She hung herself in the feed barn and they buried her under the thorn tree; the one with the swing.

Inside the envelope is the letter that introduced Jan to Mum, still sealed. Perhaps it's for the best that Mum's dead.

That afternoon I reclaim the roof room. The air is stale and the window is screwed shut. The floor is covered in boxes. There are tables and armchairs, beds and cookers made from pieces of cardboard. In the kitchen, blue cotton wool is billowing from the gas cooker. In the dining room a bloodied knife lies on the floor in a pool of red. In the sitting room a glass of wine is tipped over. The bedroom is scattered with a confetti of pills.

One box is turned over. I lift it. A cardboard man lies in the bath with an electric fire. It's not horrifying.

I clear the room, stuffing the cardboard into bin-bags and spraying every surface with disinfectant. I take a screwdriver to the window but it's stuck. I hammer it open. A herring gull lurches into the air with a piercing shriek. I'll give the place a clean coat of paint ready for Eddie's return and stock up with fish fingers and frozen waffles for the children. I'll put out bread for the gulls. And when things have settled, I'll plant a tree out the back, something quick growing like a silver birch, where I can hang a swing

MY LOBOTOMY

Barney Walsh

Jade decided to forgive me after all, just like she always did, so when she had a quiet moment at work – she's a checkout girl at a little corner supermarket – she sent me a text telling me so. I never read it. She kept glancing at her mobile, hoping for a reply, but nothing came. It wasn't like me not to call Jade, of all girls, straight back. Because I loved her, I really did. She knew that. She sent me another text, paranoid that *I* didn't know: *Aids, love u btw.* I never got that one, either. I'd thrown my phones in the canal.

Jade beeped and bagged people's shopping, taking their money and feeding them lottery tickets. Lonely women dragging screaming kids, lechy blokes trying to flirt with her, she just laughed at them. Other men seemed kind of pathetic and inadequate next to me, next to her Aids (only my aunt called me *Aidan*), she'd told me so and I believed her. The kids made her think of my lost child, though, the one I'd got rid of (Jade could've been its stepmum, she kept thinking). All the while she was working, Jade fretted and wondered why I wasn't replying, if only to say *fuck off* if I didn't want to forgive her yet in return. She decided I was just being a bit of a twat, had no inkling yet of what I'd done to myself.

After her shift was done, Jade went home to shower and change before coming looking for me at the squat I'd lived in for the past year. Lived in and dealt from – I sold drugs, Jade didn't love it but she didn't mind deeply. Like I said, she'd forgive me anything. But I wasn't there to forgive, this time. She knocked on the door – she'd got a key, but didn't know if it was still okay to use it – only to be told I'd gone, back to my aunt and uncle's house, where I'd grown up but hadn't been for years.

'What?' said Jade. 'No, he'd *never*. He never would. He *hates* them, always has. They're what fucked him up in the first place, he told me.'

'He has, though,' said Sonia. 'I couldn't believe it either at first but that's what he's done. I followed him to make sure, saw him go in. He hugged his mum or his aunt or stepmother or his nan or whatever she is. This grey-haired old woman. Gave her a big hug, right there on the doorstep. They were both crying. I've never seen Aids cry before, it were dead weird. I waited ages, but he never come out.'

Sonia was the mother of my lost child, the one I'd got shut of. She stood there in the squat's dark front room – boards over the windows – wearing nothing but her bra and denim miniskirt, and the track marks of all her life's heroin injections, every grain of it sold her by me, all up her arms. Our baby had been born addicted to heroin, which had seemed kind of hilarious at the time. Sonia told Jade how I'd disappeared – her fingers twisting about one another, pipe-cleaners worn smooth – how she'd pleaded with me not to go, clung to my leg so that I'd had to smack her one across the face. I'd never hit Jade, but sometimes Sonia had needed to be told things, like when she was on at me for free samples. It was weird that I'd not been much bothered by Jade never wanting to taste any.

Jade said, 'And you just let him go?'

In the gloom behind Sonia, sunken eye-deep in the wheezy cracked couch was Mickey. What's left of him.

'*Let* him?' went Mickey's wheezy cracked voice. 'Tried to stop him, didn't we, Sonia? But he wasn't having it. He'd decided. You can't make Aids do anything he don't want to. He'd *decided*. He's gone back to his wicked stepparents, or whatever they are. You won't see him again.'

'They're his aunt and uncle, I think,' said Jade. 'They adopted him. Or something.'

'Whatever, he's theirs again now. Gone straight, he has. Collar and tie. The only one who could've stopped him, Jade, is *you*,' said Mickey. 'And where were you? You'd only gone and ditched him, hadn't you? So don't you tell *us* for letting him go.'

Mickey didn't like Jade because she wouldn't let him fuck her. Up till she'd dumped me, I fucked Jade mostly and Sonia occasionally – less with Sonia lately than I'd used to, since Jade'd stopped being jailbait – and other girls too, often; but Mickey fucked no one, basically. Only himself. It was only that one time that I'd let him suck me off, which'd turned out to be a mistake.

'I don't believe this,' said Jade.

'It was dead odd,' said Sonia. 'Like, before he went he told us *sorry*, me and Mickey – he, like, *apologised* for what he said he'd done to us.' (It was true: I had done that. For whatever worth *sorry* is.) 'I didn't know what he was on about,' said Sonia.

'Look yourself in the mirror,' said Mickey. 'You'll figure it out.'

Jade didn't say anything.

Sonia asked, 'Did he … like, did he tell *you* sorry too?'

'No,' Jade said. 'He's not said a thing about this to me.'

'What'd you break up with him for?'

'Doesn't matter.'

'I'd thought … when you two ended, I thought maybe he'd come back to *me*, but he never…' Sonia started to cry. 'I couldn't stop him,' she said. 'He's gone for *ever*. I've *lost* him.'

She went and folded herself headfirst into an armchair's arms, curled there crying. Sonia'd always believed that somehow we'd get our baby back, as if I'd ever let that happen. Now I was gone, too.

'You'd *already* lost him,' Jade said, feeling a need to be cruel. 'He was *mine*, not yours – not since *ages* ago.'

'Not any more,' said Mickey. 'He's no one's now. He's his fucking *auntie and uncle's* again now. *You* let him go.' Mickey leant forward to the table, gathering the bits to cook up with. 'Join us for once?' he said, his eyes on Jade's breasts. I'd have broken his nose for that look, if I was still myself, still the old Aids, still there.

'No way,' Jade said. 'I'm going to get him back.'

It might not be too late, she thought. She could go find me, tell me she forgives me, beg me to forgive her, get me back again. If *only* she'd not dumped me... She couldn't believe it, I'd gone back to my aunt and uncle! My fucking foster parents or whatever they were. I hated them, I'd told her often enough, not seen them in *years*. *They're dead to me*, I'd said when Jade asked once. And now I'd gone back to them. To get clean, sober, safe, sane – to get *normal*. I'd be getting a *job* next, and then … and then Jade had a sudden sick feeling that I might have done something worse to myself, if I'd suddenly decided I wanted to be like everybody else, if being the Aids who Jade loved was so doing my head in. She had to move fast.

'Yeah,' said Sonia. 'Yeah, you can save him.'

Jade knew where my aunt and uncle lived because I'd once shown her, pointed it out and sat on a garden wall at the end of the road and told her stories of how I hated them, mostly invented on the spot but she couldn't know that. They weren't my parents, my real mum and dad were ghosts before I was born, and they weren't even really my aunt and uncle, not blood at all (or maybe my uncle was – someone'd once drawn a spidery family tree on the back of an envelope but it'd been lost long ago). They'd brought me up, I hated them. I told Jade this, some true things and some lies. Her body folded into mine, my arm around her, her thigh against my leg, her head leant on my chest looking up, over my heart, wide darkly eye-linered eyes looking up at me. Jade. These things lost.

Jade headed off out from the squat fast but Sonia came clattering after her in her heels, still buttoning the top she'd thrown on. Mickey stayed behind, shooting up. When they got to my aunt's street, a nice suburban road, tree-lined, far posher than where Jade lived, Jade told Sonia to wait 'cause she looked too much of a mess, let Jade sort this out alone. She went through my uncle's front garden and rang the doorbell. After a bit it opened.

'Hiya,' Jade said, friendlyishly trying to sound normal and safe. 'Can Aids come out to play?'

My so-called aunt, Auntie Linda, not a blood relation, short grey hair, her thin face's sags held together by wrinkles like wires, old-enough-looking to be my grandma, not just my adopted mother. She gave Jade a long, slow up-and-down look before saying, 'You'll be that Jade, then, won't you?'

'That's me, yes.' Jade smiled. 'Is he in, please?'

'You don't know, do you not?'

'Don't know what?'

'He's not here, love. Didn't he tell you? Thought you of all girls'd be the first to know. He's round the hospital having his head fixed.'

'Oh. Right.'

He can't have, Jade thought. He can't really've gone and *done* it. But I had.

'Maybe he wanted to surprise you,' Linda said, eyeing over Jade's shoulder Sonia hanging about waiting in the street, standing there pretending she was invisible, hopping from foot to foot, looking like exactly what she was. 'Or maybe he didn't tell you so you couldn't talk him out of it. Maybe he knew you were the only one who could've stopped him going through with it, and that's why he didn't tell you.'

'Uh, right ... so, um, when'll he be back?'

My aunt titled her head to look down her nose at Jade, though really they were eye-level, making it clear she was *nothing* to her, not now she'd got her precious boy, me, out of Jade's clutches.

'Tomorrow, all being well,' Auntie Linda said, closing the door. 'Tomorrow he'll be himself again, not the thing *you* made him.'

'I *never*, he was like that when I met him –'

But the door was shut.

Shit. Jade got out of there, the gate's hinges squeaking again.

Sonia whined, 'He's not come *with* you…'

'No,' Jade said. 'We're too late, he's not here. He's at the hospital, having his brain worked on.'

'His brain?'

'They're making him the safe, normal human being he's always secretly wanted to be.'

'Oh,' said Sonia. 'Oh, right. It's like what he said, then.'

'What is?'

'Aids said. Before he ran off. He's trying to save his soul, he is.'

And standing there Sonia started crying, silently weeping, she stood there with her fists clenched at her little skirt's hem, her thin bare arms all run up and down with old self-harm scars and the fresher marks of her drug habits. Tears made her dark eye makeup leak down her face like the roots leaking from her blonde-dyed hair. Jade watched her for a minute. She felt a sudden rush of hate, and then of love – and then she wandered off.

*

The hospital's glossy brochure had been pushed through the squat's front door a month or so earlier, with a note saying something like *We'll pay, you can be made all better, we forgive you and love you, love from Auntie Linda & Uncle Derek*. I had glanced at it, snorted, tossed it into a corner. Jade should have destroyed it, torn it to pieces, burnt it – because she realised now that I must have gone back and found it, later, sat down and had a good read. And decided. I'd tried to kill myself before, twice that Jade knew of. Once before she met me, once when she'd been the one to find me. She'd come round my place after school and stopped me dying, that'd been only about the third time we'd had sex, a couple of years ago, fucking in the bathtub into which my slashed wrists were spilling blood. Fucking her, her legs about me, not dead yet, I'd held my hand in her hair as if blessing her and watched my blood flow down her face, her breasts. And now instead I was laid out on a slab in the hospital with my brains dribbling over some surgeon's fingers...

It wasn't like I'd ever done anything really bad, Jade thought. Only, like, bits and pieces of badness. Drug-dealing, above all else – and also burglary once or twice, stealing cars a few times, a mugging or two, attempted blackmail that time, receiving stolen goods, smuggling (yeah, really), and okay yes statutory rape multiple times with Jade herself but she'd outgrown that so it didn't really count, did it? Just that once, GBH that wasn't really my fault – my crimes almost all not violent when they didn't need to be (though they often *did* need to be, it seemed). And whatever I'd done, Jade loved me. Poor sweet not-so-vulnerable Jade, seventeen now but still a child really, more mature than I'd ever been, Jade loved me. She thought of me, remembering my blood on her face, as she walked home from my aunt's house. How would Jade have described me, the me I'd been? Mad bad sad crazy unpredictable beautiful up-and-down clever witty morality-less dangerous sexy manic-depressive violent nutter borderline-suicidal artistic hooligan alcoholic smackhead drug-dealing talented lovely lonely sweet handsomeish-in-a-bonily-ugly-kind-of-way vulnerable carefree perverted gloomy mood-swingy punk skinhead head-the-ball indescribable inventive witty genius lunatic conman poet artist Aids, always called Aids (funny story behind the nickname, one best told in A & E waiting rooms, I've found) though my dotted-line name (that never got on anyone's dotted line, not till I signed myself in at the hospital), is Aidan followed by a surname that I never tell anyone.

Jade went home. Her mum'd made tea. She asked why Jade was so quiet. Jade said it's nothing. Her mum said okay, and looked knowing.

*

A few days later, in her dinner break, Jade's mobile rang. She didn't recognise the number, answered it all unsuspecting, and it was that woman again, my wicked stepmother saying, 'Well, Aidan's home now. Right as rain all over again. Like he's been born again, you should see him. In fact, you *should* see him. We think that's a good idea, just for you to see he doesn't need you any more, and for him to see what he's well rid of. How does that sound? Pop round this afternoon, all right? We'll have a cup of tea, chat over old times, how they'll never be repeated because you're not going to be part of the new times, not so far as my boy's concerned.'

She hung up. And Jade knew what had to be done. This was her last chance. She had to do everything she could to get me out of my aunt's clutches. Jade told her supervisor she wasn't feeling well, the super looked sceptical, Jade mentioned my name and the woman shuddered. Jade hurried home, shaved her legs, showered and changed, got dressed carefully sexily to lure me off from them, to let me know soon as I set eyes on her that I'd be fucking her shortly if only I'd come home with her. A tiny skirt, boots with heels, strapless top under her jacket. Red on the lips and dark on the eyes. Not exactly subtle. She could do this. It wasn't too late. I could still be saved, Jade had to believe.

But walking round there again she couldn't help imagining what was waiting for her: me with my head all shaven, shiny-bald and peppered with stubble, fat red worm of scar running from one temple round the back of my skull, pinkly puckered lips of it held weepingly together by thick black marker-pen stitches. The wound where they'd got at my brain, removed the bad, made me someone else.

Jade rang the doorbell again. *Remember*, she thought as she waited, *he loves me*. The door opened faster this time: the same woman, Linda, my unloving stepaunt, smiling a pretend smile, a disguise meant to be seen through.

'Come in, dear,' she said, acting as if this was her meeting her son's or nephew's girlfriend for the first time, as if all this were normal and happy. She ushered Jade through to a nice bland living room, plaster ducks on the wall – God, *really*? – brass oddments about the fireplace. Jade didn't see yet what was sitting on the mantelpiece. 'Aidan will be down in a minute,' my aunt said. 'I'll just get the tea things, you make yourself comfy, dear.'

Jade sat. Her eyes glanced about the room, passing over the glass jar without seeing what it was. She waited. The woman came back, set a tea tray on the table, teapot and cups and dainty milk jug and sugar bowl. *Do people really do this?* Linda poured Jade a cup of tea, said help yourself to sugar, went away again and when she came back she brought me with her, holding my hand.

'Aids?' Jade said, but I didn't answer, seemed not to hear or understand, just shuffled forwards, led by my aunt.

There was no scar on my head: maybe they'd not really done it, Jade thought. But then she saw how I was.

'Aids, look at yourself,' she said. 'You've gone all *zombified*.'

I was wearing a white, neatly pressed shirt, all buttoned up, wrists and throat, and grey trousers that looked like school uniform. I was twenty-seven, thin and wirily muscled, but even in that body I looked to Jade now like a six year old. My head hung low from my shoulders, my eyes fallen on the carpet. One hand held loosely the other's wrist. My toes pointed inwards, a bit. There was a coin-sized darkish patch, nestled in my crotch. Oh my God, Jade thought. My head wasn't shaved – it'd been shaved before, but now it had a month's thickening of stubble. There was no scar that Jade could see. As my aunt sat me carefully down Jade rose and stepped around me, to check the other side of my head.

They go in through the eyes, explained my aunt. And look, they're not even bruised. Wonders they work nowadays. They'd popped them out onto my cheeks, left them dangling there, looking at not a lot, while they stuck their chisels deep up into my dripping sockets.

My lower lip had gone bigger than it used to be, wetly bulging at one side. One eyelid drooped weirdly, sometimes twitched a bit and then calmed and re-drooped itself.

'He's drooling,' Jade said, pointing. 'Look, he's fucking *drooling.*'

'It's just a little,' said Auntie Linda. She plucked a tissue from her sleeve, went and dabbed at my chin. 'He'll soon get used to it. The doctor says he has to learn some things again, that's all.'

'*Like being able to close his lips?*' Jade almost shouted.

'I won't have language in this house, thank you,' Aunt Linda said. 'You're only here on sufferance, you know.'

'I can't fucking believe this is happening,' Jade said, sinking her face in her hands.

'Look,' my auntie said. '*Look.*'

Jade lifted her head and followed my aunt's pointing finger. And there it was, on the mantelpiece, in what looked like an old coffee jar, the bit of my brain that they'd removed – it's my brain so I get to keep it, what else would they do with it? – sat there sunk to the bottom of its jar, in clear liquid already faintly discolouring. Pale flesh brownly darkening in the coiled lobes' creases.

Jade said, 'Oh. My. Fuck. Ing. God.'

My aunt said, 'Do you know what that is? That's *you*, Jade. That's *you*, excised from my boy Aidan's life. You, and the badness that poisoned his soul, cut from his mind and from him for *ever.*'

'What've you *done* to him?!'

'What he *wanted.* It was his own decision, you must know that. You think we can have *forced* him into anything he didn't want? This was *his* choice. He took himself to our GP, got a referral to the hospital. Was always early for his appointments. He couldn't go on being what he was: a criminal, an addict, a pimp for all I know…' – giving Jade again one of those up-and-down *disgusted* looks. 'And his bipolarity. He couldn't cope with another pit of it, that's what he said, so he came to us, to his auntie and his uncle – to his *parents* – and got away from you. From *you.*'

'It's because I dumped him,' Jade said. 'If I'd not done that then –'

'Lie to yourself as much as you like. He couldn't go through another bout like before. And *you* were no help, only made him worse.'

'He just wanted to die,' Jade said. 'That's all he's done, he's let you kill him for him.'

'You know *nothing* about my boy. The part that's addicted is gone. The part that's addicted to *you* is gone.'

'Why doesn't he talk for himself?'

'He's just adjusting, it'll take a while, like I said. He's got a job, too.'

'A job?' said Jade. 'Doing what? Aids's never had a proper job in his life. You'll be telling me next he's going to start paying *taxes.*'

'Well he *is*. He's learning a trade, going to be a plumber, he's got an apprenticeship, his uncle – his *father* wangled it for him. He starts Monday. On Sunday we're in church, to pray thanks for our boy's return. So you see he doesn't need you any more. I just wanted you to be sure of that. Now, then, what about that tea?'

*

When my trembling, unmanageable hands slopped tea onto the table, my aunt went to the kitchen for a cloth to mop it with. Once she was gone Jade jumped into the armchair with me.

'Quick,' she whispered. '*Now*, while she's not looking, come on, let's *go*, let's get *out* of here.'

I said nothing, just sat there rolling my eyes at the floor. When she tried to put her arms around me I leaned away instinctively out of her grasp, my lips soundlessly moving.

'Come *on*,' Jade said in my ear. 'Listen, *I love you*. And I *know* you love me. Whatever it is they've done to you, I'll make it right. I *promise*. Just let's get out of here. *Now*.'

I managed some sounds: 'Nuh-uh' – shaking my head, shaking my head.

'Fuck sake, use *words*. Come on, we have to leave. *Now*. *Please*, Aids. Come back to me. I *love* you.'

But all I could do was hang my head at the floor. I shut my eyes, pretending Jade wasn't there. So she stuck her hand down my pants, found my dick – *that* they'd not cut off, not yet – and with the other hand she turned my head and forced my eyes to meet hers – but there was nothing she could see in there, and nothing she could feel moving, not a twitch.

'I think you should go now.'

My aunt returned. Jade looked at me desperately.

'Aids, please!'

And I managed a bit more: 'Luh-uh … luh-*leave* me alone!'

'Time to go, dear.'

She led Jade through to the hall, me shuffling after them, barely knowing what was going on, on my way upstairs for a nap, I got overtired so easily, my aunt said. She opened the door for Jade.

'Goodbye. We won't be seeing you again, I don't think.'

'Aids…' Jade said. 'I'm sorry.'

'His name's *Aidan*,' my aunt spat. 'He's not named after a *disease – you're* the only disease in his life!'

Jade ignored her, made one last try, she flowed her body into mine, with her arms around my neck she pulled my face down to hers, tried to kiss me but I moved my head automatically away and her lips slipped uselessly off a patch of drool on my chin. I stepped backwards away from her as if frightened, though there still wasn't really any emotion Jade could see on my face. Only vacancy. She stood there uselessly, arms empty.

'See?' said my aunt. 'He's not yours any more. And just *look* at you. All got up like a slut. Do you honestly expect I'd let *my* son give his life to the likes of *you*?'

'No,' Jade said quietly.

'*No*. You'd best go now.'

Jade looked at her, hating her, looked at the big oblong blankness of the open door, of never-again. And said, 'Hang on, I forgot my bag.'

She darted quickly back into the living room, grabbed her bag from where she'd left it under the coffee table, stepped to the fireplace and quick as *that* the jar was off the mantelpiece and into her bag, she zipped it shut, dashed back into the hall. Neither me nor my aunt – the one half-brainless, the other old – had had time to move.

'Okay, sorry, I'll be off now.'

Jade got outside, down the garden path for the last time to the gate, walked quickly up the street and away, feeling the door held open behind her, watching her suspiciously, till she rounded the street's far corner and it was safe to burst into tears.

She'd lost me, she really had. The madman she'd loved was gone and dead, for ever. And she'd loved me. Amazing to realise. She stood there crying for a long time, but time passes and nothing goes backwards, and eventually she had to go home.

*

Jade had stolen back my brain for me but now that it was hers she had no idea what to do with it. She didn't think she could just *keep* it, much as she'd like to – you have to say goodbye, don't you? She'd loved me but now I was gone. It wasn't like she could push my brain into hers, like through her ear, merge her mind with mine. If only. Or if like she ate it. Slice it up, fry it in butter, watch its raw inner pinkness turn dark, nicely browning, flip it to the other side with a fork, hot oil spitter-spatter, bubblingly frying in its own juices. Done to a turn. Mopping up my last cerebral crumbs with a bit of bread. How would it taste? *Like … like his cock, Aids's brain'd taste just like his cock*, Jade thought … though of course no it wouldn't.

She flashed back to those times, me in her mouth, her maybe still in school uniform, the pressure of my hands on her moving head. The taste of me. Who'd have thought cannibalism could be so mouth-wateringly tempting? *Tempting* ... but no – the cooking would burn up the memories, my last frozen thoughts, the shadow of my love for Jade all fried and destroyed. They wouldn't last into her mouth. And she couldn't eat my brain *raw*, that'd just be *gross*.

So what she thought she'd do is have herself a little private funeral. Just her and me, the little of me she still had, to say her goodbyes. At night, in a sunset's dying glow. We'd watched a sunset or two in the years we'd been together, passing between us a spliff – the limit of what she'd touch of my drugs, but I'd not minded that after at first, when she was a thirteen-year-old schoolgirl and I'd tried and failed to get her hooked on heroin. Pissed me off that I couldn't do it but soon I was all good-humoured again. There weren't many girls could ever say *no* to me, the old me, Jade was one of the few. She was never going to be just another girl. We'd watched literally only a couple of sunsets, but they'd happened. I never complained that Jade was holier than me on the drugs score, she wasn't like that, she just didn't want any. I never tried to spike her drink or anything. That one time it happened, it wasn't me – that's what Jade believed. She did believe me after a bit, she didn't at first, but now she does forever. There was one sunset in particular that had nakedly bathed us in honey as we ever-so-gently fucked (it was never normally gentle), and that magical moment was one of the pearls of Jade's memory (though it'd pretty much slipped *my* mind even before the knife had slipped through my mind), so she decided that'd be the spot to bury me, the bit of me that was hers to bury – till it occurred to her what about little animals trying to dig me up, make off with and gobble me up themselves. It wasn't like she'd be able to dig very deep. Couldn't be having *that*. So she decided she'd cremate me. At night, up on the heath, alone, she'd build a bit of a pyre out of twigs, have a bottle of something, say goodbye with a little crying, a little irreligious funeral ceremony all on her own, no words said. On the weekend, if it didn't rain.

*

When she got home she stuck the chunk of my brain that she'd stolen in its jar on top of her chest of drawers, in her bedroom. If my aunt sent the police round – if she even knew where Jade lived – after her stolen property, Jade could always flush it down the toilet: it was only turd-sized anyway, this small cylinder of my grey matter. In certain ways that'd be kind of fitting, considering the amount of time in my life that I'd spent with my head in the bowl. In the meantime Jade tried not to think about me. Saved up all her thoughts for that funeral session. But she couldn't help my old face floating up in her mind, and the ruin of what they'd done to me shuffling about my aunt and uncle's house. She had to do something. She called some friends, ages since they'd heard from her, they sounded wary, I'd always scared Jade's friends off, and then delighted when they heard she wasn't with me any more – though she didn't spell out what I'd done to myself.

She went out, put on a dancing dress and went and got pissed. A short dress made of a liquid metal that flowed clingingly over her body's curves. A bar, another bar, a nightclub. She went drunkenly on the pull as if she could ever find another like me, as if there might be another Aids out there for her somewhere, and not just some dickhead. But a dickhead it was that she found, this weedy lad all over Jade, crushing her boobs with his hands as he slobbered a bad impression of a kiss down the side of her face and she thought might as well but then *no* – the only man in her life she'd ever been fucked by was me, and she wasn't ready after all for that to change. She slapped away the drunken twat, went to the toilets to puke a bit, stumbled into a taxi, folded up on the back seat. Laid on her back she stared up not blinking at the streetlights floating by above her but, like, feeling as if they were far below. At a red light the driver turned to look at her, at her curled bare legs, just another drunk girl in his taxi, what did he know.

'You all right? Not gonna be sick, are you?'

'Are we there yet?' Jade asked, like a child.

The car pulled into Jade's road, she paid, let herself into the house. Her mum's voice called down, 'You all right, love?' From her bedroom, where she'd been lying awake, waiting to hear her only child come safely home again.

'Yeah, Mum,' Jade said. 'Yeah'm fine.'

'…Goodnight then, love.'

'G'night, M'm.'

She got herself into her bedroom, it was dark, she banged her knee on the bedside table. Ow. Found the light switch, changed her mind, went and opened the window's blinds to let in some moon. She kicked off her shoes and threw off her jacket, sat on the bed and cried for a bit. Her bedroom I'd never got into – we'd only ever had sex at my squat, or elsewhere, or outdoors. After a bit she lifted her face from her hands and saw herself in the mirror: her face all a mess from the tears ruining her makeup, sweaty from drinking and dancing, her hair all tousled like just-been-fucked hair but she'd *not* been fucked, her dress's strap fallen from one shoulder but no one'd touched it, no one'd touched her, all it'd done was fall. In the dim moonlight everything in the room and mirror looked black and white and the black spilling from her eyes might've been blood.

She saw it, then, stuck on top of the drawers, her bra from before chucked over it, in its glass jar, the small shred of my lobotomised brain, pale flesh faintly glowing in the slats of moonlight that slipped through the blinds.

She wanted me back. She wanted her Aids back. She loved me. She jumped up, grabbed the jar, brought it back to bed with her, sat there cross-legged with its glass cupped coldly between her bare thighs. Tomorrow she'd burn it, she thought. Have a little cremation. Say goodbye properly. She could see it already in her head, the fire, more perfect of course than it'd turn out to be in real life. Up on the heath, in the sunset, the fire's yellow pale against the richer colour of the sunset, rising heat turning things glassily warped, the way fires do, the sunset sinking into a starry night's upward depths, if not romantically sliced by a shooting star or two then at least a little chain of Chinese lanterns, small distant orangey fires floating up and away from someone else's party, someone else's love.

She was crying again. Probably on the real night it'd rain, the fire wouldn't get going; probably on the real day it'd be crap. But we'd see. We'd see, but for right now she was just so alone, lonely for me, lonely for Aids, the me she loved and had lost. No matter how bad I got sometimes, how psychotic or depressed, she'd loved me. She unscrewed the jar's lid, dipped her fingers into the cold fluid inside, pulled out the shred of flesh. The part of my brain that I'd loved her with. She held it in her hand, soft cold flesh, a pale strip of cerebral matter maybe a couple of inches long. She cupped it in her palms, rolled it between her fingers, breathed on it, trying to warm it again, ran her fingers over its smooth, rubbery lobes. She held it tenderly to her cheek, all that she had left of me, kissed it lightly a peck and then more slowly. She missed me. The man I'd been. She saw me still in her head, how I'd been before I'd had this terrible thing done to me, she saw my face from before, my hands on her, my breath on her skin, my lips on her body, myself inside her, it was all still there, and then in one quick sudden thoughtless movement she rolled onto her back, wriggled her knickers off, parted her thighs and slipped the piece of my brain up inside herself. She gasped. Slowly and then faster she fucked herself with it, with her fingers and my flesh, this last small part of me that was hers, the chunk of my brain the surgeons'd so cruelly cut from me, she rubbed it against her clit and felt the brain's flesh swelling as its little dregs of blood, its paltry stored chemical memories, began to move again, its thoughts' neurons to spark again, warming as the blood started once more to flow.

Fuck me, Jade thought. *Come on, fuck me. You think you're dead, I'll fucking show you.* And she felt it happening as I fucked her from beyond the grave, from beyond the grave I'd not been buried in yet, she felt me coming back to life, yes yes *yes*, all that way over there lying in my old bedroom, tucked in like a child, she knew I was stirring back into life again, the old me, waking and rising, staggering to my feet, wildly punching a wall in rage, my eyes refocusing, pouring vodka down my neck, smashing my aunt's face to the floor, setting fire to the house, yanking some poor bastard from his car, taking it, coming for Jade, wreaking devastation on all before me, angrier than ever, more lost than ever, heading out with the dawn's sky aglow to find her, she could see it, as she pressed my pulsing brain up into her cunt she knew, yes, that I was coming back to her, yes, that I was still alive, alive again, and coming back to her.

UNTHOLOGISTS

Elizabeth Baines second collection of short stories is due from Salt this summer. Her first collection, *Balancing on the Edge of the World*, and two novels, *Too Many Magpies* and *The Birth Machine*, are also published by Salt.'. Individually, her stories have been published in numerous magazines and anthologies including *Red Room: New Short Stories Inspired by the Brontës*, *Best British Short Stories 2014*, and have won prizes, most recently in the 2014 Short Fiction Journal Prize. Her story *Clarrie and You* appeared in *Unthology 5*. She has also written prizewinning plays for radio and stage.

Roelof Bakker lives in London. He is the founder of Negative Press London and editor of *Still* (Negative Press London, 2012). *Strong Room*, a collaboration with artist Jane Wildgoose, was published in 2014. 'Red' appears in *Unthology 5* (Unthank Books, 2014) and 'Blue' in *Unthology 6* (Unthank Books, 2015).

Gary Budden is the co-founder of independent publisher Influx Press and works as a fiction editor for *Ambit* magazine. His fiction and creative non-fiction has appeared in *Structo*, Galley Beggar Singles Series, *Under the Radar, PUSH, Bare Fiction, Elsewhere Journal, The Quietus* and many more. He writes regularly for the website Unofficial Britain. His Annexe Introducing pamphlet, 'Tonttukirrko' was published in 2014.

Elaine Chiew is a London-based writer, and her short stories have won the Bridport Prize (2008), *Camera Obscura's* Bridge- the-Gap competition (2010), been shortlisted for the 2014 MsLexia Prize, and been shortlisted twice for the Fish Short Story Prize (2012). They have also been selected by Dzanc Books' Best of the Web (2008), Wigleaf's Top 50 Microfiction (2008), storySouth's Million Writers Award (Top 10 Winner, 2006), the Per Contra Prize (Top 10 Winner, 2008) and *Glimmer Train's* Top 25 Emerging Writers Competition (2005). They've also appeared in numerous publications, including *One World: A Global Anthology* (New Internationalist, 2009) and *Short Circuit: Guide to the Art of the Short Story* (Salt, 2009). She is the editor and organizer of a new anthology *Cooked Up*: Food Fiction Around the World (publication in March 2015). She blogs about food and fiction on redemptioninthekitchen.blogspot.com

Adrian Cross lives in London. He is a graduate in Philosophy and works with children in care. He has contributed to the *Times Educational Supplement* and writes music reviews. In 2011 he was runner up in The Guardian's Travel Writing Competition. He has completed the MA in Creative Writing at Goldsmiths College and had short fiction published in *Dreamcatcher*. He is currently working on two novels, an urban comedy and a slice of fen noir.

George Djuric flew through rally racing, street fighting, chess, and anti-psychiatry as if they weren't there. In the aftermath, all that was left was writing. He published a critically acclaimed collection of short stories, a book read like the gospel by his Yugoslav peers, *The Metaphysical Stories*. Djuric is infatuated with the fictional alchemy that is thick as amber and capable of indelibly inscribing on the face of the 21st century. He lives in the desert near Palm Springs, CA.

Ken Edwards' most recent book is *Down With Beauty* (Reality Street, 2013). Others include *Bardo* (Knives Forks and Spoons Press, 2011) and *No Public Language: Selected Poems 1975-1995* (Shearsman Books, 2006). He runs the small press Reality Street from Hastings, where he also plays bass guitar and sings with the band The Moors. His new novel *Country Life* is forthcoming from Unthank Books.

Charlie Hill is a writer from Birmingham. He is the author of two provocative novels and numerous short stories.

Debz Hobbs-Wyatt lives and works in Essex as a full time writer and editor. She has an MA in Creative Writing from Bangor University and has had several short stories published. She has also been short listed in a number of writing competitions, including being nominated for the prestigious US Pushcart Prize 2013 for her story *The Theory Of Circles* published in *Unthology 3;* made the short list of the Commonwealth Short Story Prize 2013 and won the Bath Short Story Award 2013. Her debut novel *While No One Was Watching* was published in 2013 by Parthian Books. She edits and critiques for publishers and writers and has a daily writing Blog.
Website: debzhobbs-wyatt.co.uk
Blog: wordznerd.wordpress.com
Author Fan Page: facebook.com/DebzHobbsWyattAuthor
Twitter @DebzHobbsWyatt

Sonal Kohli grew up in Delhi and graduated from University of East Anglia MA in Creative Writing in 2013. Her stories have been published by *The Caravan, Monkeybicycle, and newwriting.net,* and she was recently awarded a Writing Fellowship at Sangam House, India. Sonal lives in Washington, D.C. with her husband.

David Martin is a journalist in the least glamorous sense and a musician in the least successful sense, from York, UK. He was shortlisted for the Big Issue In The North New Writing Award and his short fiction has previously been published by *The London Magazine,* Valley Press and Dead Ink Books. He will publish a collection of short stories, *Only Shadows Move*, in the near future. Twitter @lordsludge.

Roisín O'Donnell is an Irish writer whose work has been published in Ireland, the UK and Australia. Her family are from Derry and she grew up in Sheffield before moving to Ireland to study at Trinity College Dublin. Having taught abroad and travelled widely in Spain and South America, she is presently teaching English as an additional language at Dublin City University. She was recently shortlisted for the *Bath Short Story Award 2014* and the *Cúirt New Writing Prize 2014*, and she received and honourary mention in the *Fish Flash Fiction Prize 2014*. Her short stories and poems have appeared in *Popshot*, *Colony* and *Structo*. Further stories are due to be anthologised in *Fugue: Contemporary Stories* (The Siren), *Unfettered* (Tiny Owl, Brisbane) and in *Young Irelanders* (New Island, 2015). She lives in Dublin and is currently working on her first short story collection.

Amanda Oosthuizen is a musician and woodwind teacher living in Hampshire, UK. Her stories are published extensively online, in print and last year pasted up on the London Underground (probably legally). Recently, stories have won the 2013 Litro/Poland/Bruno Schulz and the 2014 Synaesthesia Magazine competitions, shortlisted for the 2013 Bristol Prize and runner-up in the 2014 Writers&Artists competition. She has an MA with distinction in Creative Writing from the University of Chichester where she was joint winner of the 2010 Kate Betts Memorial Prize. She has written several novels, which are all currently simmering on her hard drive. More details at www.amandaoosthuizen.com

Dan Powell is a prizewinning author of short fiction whose stories have appeared in the pages of *Carve, Paraxis, Fleeting* and *Best British Short Stories*. His debut collection of short fiction, *Looking Out Of Broken Windows*, was shortlisted for the 2013 Scott Prize and is published by Salt. He procrastinates at danpowellfiction.com and on Twitter as @danpowfiction.

John D Rutter completed his MA at Lancaster University in 2012 and is currently working on a short story PhD at Edge Hill University. His stories have been published in the *Lancashire Evening Post, Five Stop Story, Synaesthesia Magazine, 330 Words* and *Unthology 5*. He is one of the organisers of *The Word* Festival in Lancashire, a past guest editor of Lancashire Writing Hub and has read his stories at various events in the North West.

Barney Walsh is a graduate of the University of Manchester's MA in creative writing. His fiction has appeared recently in *Willesden Herald: New Short Stories 7, The Big Issue in the North: Award for Short Fiction 2013, Unthology 4,* and *The Warwick Review.*